SO-BSB-964

MAR 2 6 2001

Ghosts, Gales and Gold

Also by Edward Rowe Snow

The Islands of Boston Harbor

Fantastic Folklore and Fact

Great Atlantic Adventures

Incredible Mysteries and Legends of the Sea

True Tales and Curious Legends

True Tales of Buried Treasure

GHOSTS, GALES and GOLD

Edward Rowe Snow

PILOT PRESS
LAUREL, NY

To my son-in-law
John Leonard Bicknell

Copyright © 1972 by Edward Rowe Snow

All rights reserved

No part of this book may be reproduced in any form
without permission in writing from the publisher

ISBN: 0-396-06658-5
Library of Congress Catalog Card Number: 72-3936

Printed in the United States of America
by The Cornwall Press, Inc., Cornwall, N.Y.

To order contact
Pilot Press
Post Office Box 476
Laurel, New York 11948

Manufactured in the United States of America

Introduction

This present volume combines three subjects that have fascinated me from my earliest days—ghosts, gales and gold. As an ideal setting for reading this book, I suggest a home along the coast when wintry storms are pushing the waves of the mighty ocean high against the headlands. There, sit down in front of a roaring, crackling fire and open this volume.

I wish to express my gratitude to the Ventress Memorial Library, Marshfield; the Allen and the Peirce Memorial Libraries of Scituate; the Boston Athenaeum; the Boston Public Library; the Thomas Crane Public Library of Quincy; the Harvard College Library; the Bostonian Society; the Society for the Preservation of New England Antiquities; the Massachusetts Archives; the Peabody Museum; the American Antiquarian Society in Worcester; the Essex Institute; the Massachusetts Marine Historical League; the National Archives; the Boston Marine Society; the Massachusetts Historical Society; the Maine Historical

Society; the Nathan Tufts Library in Weymouth; and *Yankee* magazine.

I shall always remember the kindness of those who have given their ability and their time. They include the following: Dorothy Caroline Snow Bicknell, Laura Ann Bicknell, Jack Beasley, Mary Brown, Frederick G. S. Clow, Frederick M. Cochrane, Arthur J. Cunningham, James Douglas, Walter Spahr Ehrenfeld, Nina Ehrenfeld, George M. Fallon, Leo Flaherty, Edward B. Garside, Marie Hansen, Barbara Hayward, Melina Herron, Ron Knight, Joseph Kolb, Gary Kosciusko, William McIntire, Walter P. McNaney, Maggie Mills, Joel O'Brien, William Pyne, Elva Ruiz, Mrs. Carlton Rutledge, Helen Ryan Salkowski, Grace Saphir, Donald Burnham Snow, Winthrop James Snow, Roy Wendell, and Susan Williams.

Many others should be mentioned but they have requested anonymity.

I am more than grateful for the assistance of Editor John R. Herbert of the Boston *Herald Traveler*.

My wife, Anna-Myrle, worked on many occasions through the night to help me meet deadlines, and at this time I wish to thank her.

EDWARD ROWE SNOW

Contents

PART I GHOSTS

New Haven's Ship in the Sky

Everyone has come across weird cloud formations high in the heavens, resembling people and ships. And stories of phantom ships and deserted vessels have always appealed to the imagination.

One such story concerns New Haven's ship in the sky. Three historians reported the incident: James Pierpont, Cotton Mather, and John Winthrop. There is some discrepancy in the date, for although common belief places the episode in January 1647, John Winthrop's *Journal* proves conclusively that it was January 1646, when the New Haven colonists sent their ship to England.

In the early days the New Haven settlement was considered one of the most prosperous on the entire Atlantic Coast. A goodly number of the settlers had been traders and merchants back in England and, of course, were desirous of continuing trade in the New World. For several weeks they studied the sheltered little harbor which the Indians called Quinnipiac before deciding that it was the ideal location for the town they were to name New Haven.

The harbor was situated at the mouth of the Thames River, and had the advantages of being both deep and sheltered from storms by Morgan Point and Sandy Point.

The inhabitants planned for a great future when they laid out the town. They made arrangements for a large, central square with a public market where goods of all kinds could be bought and sold. They excused expert carpenters from military service, so they could build their sturdy vessels undisturbed. The tall spruce trees that served as masts were guarded carefully, and if anyone wished to cut down a tree, the governor himself was the only one who could grant his wish. A long wharf was built out to the channel so that ships of deep draught could unload their cargoes. The town fathers even passed a law that no sea captain could throw his ballast overboard in the harbor, lest it shallow the depth of their waterway to Long Island Sound. Indeed, the industrious settlers did everything in their power to make New Haven the leading seaport of Connecticut.

Captain Lamberton of New Haven soon began making voyages up the coast to Boston and Salem and down the coast as far as Delaware and Virginia. Having explored the mainland, the intrepid mariners of Connecticut then steered their vessels right out to sea to visit Bermuda, Barbados, and many islands in the West Indies. They traded lumber, wheat, and furs for sugar, molasses, and cotton. One might think that they would have established a prosperous commerce, but expenses ran high and mistakes proved costly. For example, a Milford miller who had ground his wheat improperly, sold it to the New Haven merchants for shipment to Virginia. A short time later poorly seasoned lumber was transported to the West Indies, where it caused dissatisfaction. Because of these and other unfortunate incidents, the merchants of New Haven gradually lost their trade. They might have won it back through greater experience and better products if it had not been for the Delaware incident.

Captain Lamberton and several other men of New Haven bought land in New Jersey, and sailed to their new possession to erect houses, arrange for a trading post, and organize the area for farming. But the Swedes and the Dutch who had settlements nearby claimed that the New Haven men were infringing on their rights. When Lamberton refused to move, the two groups organized against him, and in 1642 they landed at Delaware Bay, attacked the Connecticut settlement, and captured or drove into the woods every man there. Each prisoner had to pay a heavy fine before they would release him, and Captain Lamberton, who had been captured with the other prisoners, paid the largest fine of all. Then the Swedes and Dutch burned the buildings and confiscated the goods of the new colony. When Lamberton and his men returned to Connecticut, they were poorer by hundreds of pounds.

Time and again the men of New Haven tried to persuade the other New England colonies to help them get revenge, but they never received any encouragement. Captain Lamberton returned to the Swedish settlement on the Delaware and demanded satisfaction, but his former captors merely laughed at him. Later he again tried to colonize the New Jersey area and met with similar failure. It was many years before the people of New Haven gave up hope of establishing a settlement on the Delaware River.

Their next plan was to trade with England directly. For this purpose they purchased the *Fellowship,* a ship built in Rhode Island. When it arrived in New Haven Harbor, however, it did not please its new owners. Captain Lamberton said that it was a cranky vessel and might capsize in the middle of the ocean. John Winthrop, too, later called the ship "crank-sided."

Nevertheless the *Fellowship* was made ready for the long ocean journey to England. The ship was rigged with new masts and sails and the cargo began to come aboard. And what a cargo these enterprising merchants and farmers of Connecticut had gathered—beaver skins, wheat, peas, lumber, over two hundred West India hides and an amount of silver plate! The plate came from New Haven homes where householders believed that other things were more necessary than silver. In all, when fully loaded the cargo was worth six thousand pounds, which in those days represented a very substantial sum.

But the inhabitants were faced with another danger besides their "cranky" ship. John Winthrop tells us that "this was the earliest and sharpest winter we had since we arrived in the country and it was as vehement cold to the southward as here." That "vehement cold" froze the entire harbor of New Haven, trapping the *Fellowship* at the wharf. For three long miles the sea was frozen, and the men of New Haven were again in trouble, this time because of the forces of nature. Lamberton was equal to the occasion, however, and organized a large band of ice cutters to break through to Long Island Sound.

In addition to the valuable cargo, some of the most influential people of Connecticut sailed aboard the ship. In all, about seventy persons left New Haven on the *Fellowship* with Captain Lamberton at the helm. Winthrop tells us that many of those who sailed "were of very precious account."

On the day of the sailing nearly every man, woman, and child in New Haven went down on the ice and followed the progress of the vessel as she made her way to the sound. Conversation continued between the two groups until the final stretches of ice were reached. Then the Reverend Mr. John Davenport conducted a short service in which both those on board ship and those remaining at home participated. Raising his hand in prayer, Mr. Davenport spoke in a trembling, halting manner, and uttered some strangely prophetic words to the multitude: "Lord, if it be thy pleasure to bury these our friends in the bottom of the sea, they are thine; save them!"

Then the service ended, farewells were shouted, the sails filled with the breeze, and the *Fellowship* left New Haven Bay forever. Those whose loved ones were aboard climbed to the nearest headland and watched the progress of the vessel as she tacked back and forth on her way down Long Island Sound. Finally only a tiny flash of white sail could be seen as the sun caught and held it for a brief moment, then as the darkness gathered the ship vanished from sight.

With the coming of spring, word was expected of the *Fellowship,* but the weeks passed without news of any sort. Vessel after vessel came from England, but not one captain mentioned seeing or hearing from the New Haven ship. Summer arrived, and then fall, and still there was no news. By this time many people in New Haven had begun to worry, but the more hopeful ones felt that the ship had probably been delayed by a storm, or that it might have gone ashore on some island from which the passengers would later be rescued. One by one, however, as the weeks slipped by, the people lost their hope and gave in to blind despair. They recalled the words of Minister Davenport, and the entire colony went into mourning.

Winter came and still there was no word of the *Fellowship.* Long hours in prayer and meditation were spent by the pious men and women of New Haven. They entreated with God that He grant them some indication of what had happened to the ship. Finally when the sultry days of summer were at hand, their prayers were granted.

One hot June afternoon a terrific thunderstorm hit the Connecticut shores suddenly and unexpectedly. Lightning played in the skies for over an hour, and the rain came down in torrents all the while. The thunderstorm finally passed out to sea, but the sky was still alive with heavy masses of clouds slowly changing in shape.

And then a miracle was seen to occur. An hour before sunset the clouds unmistakably gave way to a strange image high in the firmament. It was the lost ship of New Haven, floating in toward them, sailing on a cloud through the sky. The news was relayed from house to house, and soon the people were all out in the streets, staring in astonishment at the miracle taking place before their eyes. The clouds came lower and lower, and the ship sailed in so close that a man might have hurled a stone aboard her.

There was the *Fellowship,* just as she had left New Haven—her keel, masts, sails, and rigging—all exactly as they had last seen her two winters before, with the tall, powerful form of Captain Lamberton himself, sword in hand, standing erect on his quarter deck.

Then, suddenly, without warning, the topmasts blew away, to hang tangled in the rigging. The masts soon went by the board, and within a few minutes the proud vessel was reduced to a battered hulk, with masses of rigging and sail in confusion all over her. A short time afterward the *Fellowship* went over on her beam ends and sank slowly into the cloud. The populace at New Haven gazed in horror at this terrible sight. Soon nothing was left of the ship in the sky, and the voice of the Reverend Mr. Davenport was heard as he spoke to his flock:

"God has condescended to send this account of His

Sovereign disposal of those for whom so many prayers have been made."

The people, their prayers answered by the Divine demonstration in the heavens, returned to their homes, their worries and fears dispelled.

The loss of the *Fellowship* put an end to commercial enterprise in New Haven for many years and almost terminated the colony as well. Oliver Cromwell, then in power in England, offered the colonists the island of Jamaica, but they declined and turned to farming for the next few years.

Eventually they learned to forget much of the sorrow that had earlier beset them, but they never could forget the year the *Fellowship* left New Haven with all their hopes, to return in such a strange fashion a year and a half later.

II

⚓

The Phantom Fiddle

In 1707 a young Harvard graduate named Jonathan journeyed to Cape Cod, where he hoped to begin a career in the ministry. He chose the town of Eastham, where he was told the Reverend Mr. Samuel Treat might be on the verge of retiring. Having graduated from Harvard in 1669, Treat had begun preaching at the Eastham Parish three years later.* Jonathan believed that Treat would soon relinquish his pastorate and he could take over, but it didn't work out that way.

Treat suggested to the younger Harvard man that there were many parishioners living too far away to attend Sunday service, and Jonathan could ably serve the Lord by visiting them. Treat explained that in the crippled condition he now found himself, he could no longer endure riding horseback for long periods of time.

Jonathan's parents were relatively wealthy Bostonians, so he had no immediate financial worries. He accepted the

---

* Lucy Treat, a collateral descendant, died only a few years ago at Cohasset.

challenge and for a home chose a salt-box house overlooking the marshes of Nauset Beach. Soon he was galloping over the Cape Cod hills and valleys, administering to the sick and explaining difficult theological passages to those who found them hard to understand.

On occasion Jonathan returned to Cambridge to visit Alice, a young girl socially prominent in the area. One day he proposed marriage and eventually she accepted.

Alice had a definite musical talent, and often played her violin for Harvard groups in the college nearby. Considered a modern girl of her day when she married Jonathan in 1709, Alice was not averse to wearing skirts that exposed parts of her ankle and blouses that approached similar fashions in England, emphasizing her beautiful shoulders. When the couple arrived at Cape Cod and attended their first service at Samuel Treat's church, Alice attracted considerable attention from both men and women.

During her husband's periods of absence from home, lonely Alice resorted to her violin, which she had brought with her from Cambridge. Eventually the Reverend Mr. Treat thought that enough time had passed for Alice to be expecting a child, but this hope of his never materialized. When a substantial length of time had elapsed, the minister decided to suggest to several of the more forward ladies of the parish that they should visit Alice and give her what was apparently needed advice. But the months went by, the ladies carried out their visitations, and about all that happened was that Alice became more and more proficient with her violin.

Then came a period when some sea captains who had visited Jonathan for counsel began to call at his home even when he was away on long trips visiting those unable to attend church. It is said that the sailing masters had become captivated by the bewitching fiddle, and were magically drawn to the home of Jonathan by its mystical notes.

Late one afternoon young Jonathan, returning from a particularly exhausting trip to Chatham, was amazed at the sound of revelry that came from his large parlor. Dismounting, he walked to the window and looked in. There was his wife, square dancing with a sea captain in such a way that every so often her ankles were revealed. Another captain was playing the fiddle.

Putting his horse in the stable, Jonathan walked across the path and threw open the door.

The music stopped at once. The captain with whom Alice had been dancing walked to the window and began to stare out. The group of visitors shortly left, and that night Jonathan disposed of the violin.

Satisfied that with the vanishing of the fiddle, his wife might not be entertaining as much as usual, Jonathan rode away the following morning for another long-distance call in Wellfleet. Everything appeared to be satisfactory when he came back. His next trip was a four-day sojourn in Chatham. On his return he was not prepared for what transpired.

Approaching the house, he heard the strange, discordant wail of a violin. He rode up to the door, dismounted carefully, and peered inside. There was his wife, sitting demurely beside the fireplace, apparently reading the Bible!

After returning three more times to the sound of revelry which did not materialize when he entered his home, Jonathan decided to make certain his wife Alice would no longer either entertain her guests or leave the house herself. He visited a whaling center at Woods Hole in the spring of the year 1717 and purchased a dozen iron bars the thickness of a whaler's harpoon. On returning home he installed the bars in each of the three windows. Then he bought a new lock and key for the door.

Unfortunately for his sanity, on his next return he heard the fiddle and the revelry from an even greater distance than before as he approached the house. He could clearly hear the tapping feet and the screams of laughter as he neared the residence, but all stopped as he unlocked the door and strode inside. There was his wife, as before, sitting demurely alongside the great fireplace, acting as though all were well.

Evidently the sea captains were not too ignorant as to what was going on at the pastor's home, for one day when Jonathan planned a particularly long journey, this time to Boston, they arrived with a ship's carpenter an hour after the minister had left at dawn.

The month was June, and there would be much daylight ahead of them. Communicating with Alice through an open window, they explained how the carpenter would create an opening in the kitchen so cleverly designed that it could never be detected.

As the last rays of the setting sun were vanishing, the carpenter completed his task, and the sea captains showed Alice her means of escape. She agreed the exit was cleverly done, but explained that she would rather have them visit her than use the new secret door herself.

Finally the time came when preacher Treat was ready to retire. To replace him the parishioners of the church chose a less eccentric pastor than Jonathan, another Harvard graduate just out of college.

The Great Snow of 1717–18 now descended on all New England, making it impossible for weeks at a time for Jonathan to leave Alice.

One night he practically went mad, as he confessed later, and promised Alice that if she would only openly carry out her sinful activities, he would give in. What he wished was for Alice to allow him to see what she did as she did it. Alice thought it over and told him that she had not been doing any of the things he claimed, and there the matter ended.

A week later when his madness reached a peak which he could not control, he seized the girl and did away with her. Putting her body into the sepulcher-like bed, he brought in from the barn a great bale of hay, which he spread around the bed. Then, deliberately, he set fire to it.

By this time his plans were made. As the fire gained headway in the house, he went out to the barn and sat down. There, by the light of a candle, he wrote his confession.

As he finished his writing, the flames from the house ascended into the heavens. Putting his confession in a vellum pouch, he saddled his horse and was soon ready to mount. By this time the flames had completely enveloped the mansion. Giving a last look at the blazing edifice, he turned his horse in the direction of the new pastor's residence.

All went well until he reached a point one mile from the preacher's home, when his mount stumbled in a deep drift through which he was attempting to force his way. The horse fell heavily. When the beast refused to get up, Jonathan continued alone, eventually reaching his destination.

Amazed to see Jonathan because of the deep drifts, the preacher invited him into the living room, but Jonathan explained that his mission was not a social one.

"I have made a failure of this life, and wish that you receive this pouch which contains my confession. I have nothing further to say, and it will be much easier for us both if you accept this envelope and permit me to depart."

Speechless at Jonathan's remarks, the young pastor allowed the murderer to leave. Then he carefully read the confession. Jonathan had explained that his wife was to blame for everything and said he believed he had married a witch!

Just what occurred then has been discussed on the Cape for many years. The version most often accepted says that after leaving the new preacher's home, Jonathan went over to the edge of Eastham Cliffs, slid and rolled to the beach below, and then walked into the ocean waves to his death.

A second story is that Jonathan committed suicide by throwing himself into a nearby pond, while a third says he escaped to Boston, where eventually he changed his name and took a parish in what is now the West End there.

Those who searched through the ruins of Jonathan's residence never could find the remains of poor Alice. Cape Codders in later days removed the harpoon-like window bars of the burned residence and made them into chimney rests for pots and kettles, similar to those Henry David Thoreau noticed on his visit to the Wellfleet Oysterman in the year 1849.

As for the fiddle, fragments of it were found in the vellum pouch along with Jonathan's confession.

III

A Brother's Warning

Captain James Scott, an English mariner, married Mary Richardson on July 14, 1760. As Captain Scott was at sea a good part of the time, Mary went to live in Marshfield, Massachusetts, with her brother Jeffrey Richardson II and his wife.

On March 4, 1787, Mary's brother was suddenly awakened about three o'clock in the morning.

"Brother Scott has arrived and called to me," he told his wife.

"Go back to sleep," she admonished, "for it is only a dream." Jeffrey Richardson, however, was strangely troubled.

"It was more than a dream," he replied, but agreed to go back to sleep.

A short time later he heard his brother-in-law call to him again. The terror in his voice prompted Jeffrey to get up. Looking at the clock he found it was about half-past three. Dressing hurriedly, he went to the door and, when he opened it, was met by a swirling blizzard.

From the appearance of the high drifts around the house it evidently had been snowing for some time, and he noted from the northeasterly direction of the wind that it would be a fearsome night for sailors on the ocean, especially if they were off a lee beach.

Jeffrey went back to his bedroom and again awakened his wife.

"I am sorry, my dear, but I simply cannot get James from my mind. There is a great snowstorm outside from the northeast, and I am afraid that he is in serious trouble."

"What do you think you should do?" asked his wife. "It will not do any good to awaken Mary and get her to worry about it, will it?"

"No, perhaps not, but I am going to go down on the shore as soon as it gets lighter."

Jeffrey lay down without taking off his clothes and fell into a fitful sleep. About six o'clock that March morning such a mighty blast shook the building that he awakened at once and leaped to his feet. Glancing outside, he noticed that it was still snowing but by now the first gray streaks of dawn were lighting up the sky in spite of the severe storm.

Jeffrey ate a quick breakfast, said good-by to his wife, put on every storm-breaking garment he possessed, and left the house. It was a long walk to the Marshfield shore, but by seven o'clock he reached his destination.

A terrifying sight met his gaze. In every direction great masses of wreckage were strewn along the beach. Dead bodies were coming ashore, mixed in with seaweed and fragments of timbers. Other men were already exploring the beach, and Jeffrey approached one of them.

"Not a soul escaped alive," the man told Jeffrey, "and I don't think anyone was on the beach when she hit!"

"What was her name?"

"I don't know, but the lighter stuff floated ashore down near Cut River, and the quarterboard might be there. It is a terrible thing, isn't it? Not a single survivor!"

Jeffrey walked down the shore, stumbling through the wreckage and the snowdrifts, until he came upon an area where the timbers and cargo were piled three feet high. Several men were busily salvaging equipment from the surf and stowing it above the reach of the tide. Walking up to one of them, Jeffrey asked about the name of the vessel. One of the workers pointed to the south.

"We did come across fragments of the quarterboard," he explained, "but you'll have to piece them together."

Jeffrey went in search of these bits of wreckage, and soon he came across what had once been the last two letters of a word, *VA*. Continuing his hunt further, he found a section bearing the letters *I, N, E,* and *R*. The evidence was incontrovertible. Captain Scott's craft was named the *Minerva*.

Sick at heart, Jeffrey walked up and down the shore for the remainder of the morning. His wife and Mary Scott arrived at the scene shortly before noon, and he could postpone no longer telling them the terrible news, that Captain Scott had been drowned almost within the sight of his own home.

The three of them returned home in sorrow. Later the men working on the shore rescued the body of Mary's husband from the waves at low tide. Just before dark the remains of the master of the *Minerva* were carried to the church, and the family was notified shortly afterward.

Captain Scott's body was so marked by the surf that it was difficult to recognize him, but a large watch he always carried with him confirmed the identification.

This watch was kept by his widow for the remainder of her life. She moved to Essex Street in Boston shortly after the tragedy and is believed to have died there about 1820.

Her children grew and prospered, and one of them inherited the watch. It is now in the possession of Roscoe E. Scott, at present a resident of Cleveland, Ohio, from whom I was able to receive many particulars about this strange story of mental telepathy and death.

Jeffrey Richardson was never able to prove that his brother-in-law spoke to him at the time of his wreck, although he was always very impatient in later years with those who questioned his story.

IV
⚓

Ghosts of Annapolis

No town of its size in this country contains more quaint old houses than Annapolis, the capital of Maryland. The area on both sides of the Chesapeake Bay is rich in folklore. Ghost historian Charles Skinner tells us that at the turn of the century, if it were not for the drilling and skylarking in the Naval Academy and the often tardy meetings of the legislature, drowsy Annapolis every now and then would have been in danger of oversleeping. Indeed, even in this year of 1972 it is a location not only of lawmakers and future admirals, but of ghosts, some of whom belong just as much to the wharves, markets, and old mansions as do the white porticoes and brass knockers so plentiful in this venerable Maryland settlement.

There is the headless man, for instance, who frequents the market-house and has been seen within a dozen years if we are to believe an ancient mariner. This sailor recalls hearing the tale about a fisherman who in 1873 left his house at three o'clock one morning to sail with the tide. Suddenly he was startled to see a man walk down Green

Street and loiter about the empty place where the garden-
ers and hucksters would presently gather, holding his head
comfortably like a football under his arm. The startled seaman turned his back on the apparition and ran home with
all his might. Arriving at his residence, the fisherman was
about to tell his wife of his unusual experience when he
found the unbelievable ghost waiting for him on his door-
step. Running around to his back door, the sailor hurriedly
took the key from its hiding place, unlocked the door, and
ran up to his bedroom. He told his wife what he had seen.
When she saw how upset he was, she threw on her robe
and quickly ran to the front door, with her husband following at a respectful distance. By this time signs of dawn
were showing, and they both went out on the porch. After
a thorough survey she saw nothing out of the ordinary.
Looking him in the eye said, "Man without a head? Nonsense!" They never discussed the matter again.

Then there was the gentle ghost at the Brice House,
which was said to have a fifty-thousand-dollar wine cellar.
This apparition, a female, never groaned, glared, or
knocked at doors and windows as ill-bred spirits often do.
Appearing at dusk, just before candles were lighted, at
the time when the rooms were vague and shadowy, she
seemed in search of someone. She looked into the faces of
those she met, then turned sadly, as though accustomed to
being disappointed, and went to the great mantel in the
parlor to lean against it with her face in her hands. As
soon as the candelabras were illuminated the ghost vanished. Her visits may have had something to do with a
fabulous treasure said to be secreted in the walls, but it
was never found.

A whitewasher in the Brice mansion, working in the
cellar in 1887, was paying particular attention one day to
a loose stone in the basement. Suddenly it swung as if it

were hinged, disclosing the entrance to a hiding place. Rolling up his sleeve so that he could thrust his arm more easily into the cavity, he stretched forth his hand just as a spider of monstrous size and horrific aspect leaped into the opening. Its head was as large as a baby's. When the whitewasher noticed the ferocious fangs, he struck at the spider with his paint-brush. The creature bit the handle in two as one might snap off a clay pipe with his teeth, and swallowed it. Terribly frightened, the workman pushed the stone back into its place, convinced that if the hiding place held money, it was not for him.

Another account of a ghost in Annapolis concerns an ancient hip-roofed Chandler mansion on Duke of Gloucester Street.* The mansion was the residence of a woman who was always held in respect for her courage and sense. Both of these qualities were put to the test one moonlight night, just after she had retired. Relaxing comfortably in her canopy bed, she was startled by the swaying of the curtains. A man then entered her bedroom.

As she explained later, she should have fainted. If she had been more sensible, she admitted, she would have thrown a pillow at him and screamed for him to get out. However, she neither screamed nor fainted. Her first thought was that he was a thief, but she soon changed her mind, for as the seconds became minutes she realized that his bearing was that of a gentleman. His actions were not furtive or menacing, and he was well dressed. Then, as the light of the moon fell across him, he bowed his head in grief. A short time later he stood up, looked sadly down the street toward a light that twinkled in an upper window of the house where her cousin lived.

---

* Although Mrs. Carleton Rutledge of Historic Annapolis, Inc. has done research concerning this mansion, she finds no evidence that a hip-roofed Chandler building ever existed.

The man gave no attention to the woman in the canopied bed nor to the objects in the room. Her next thought, therefore, was that the unknown was a visitor of distinction, possibly the guest of a great man in the town. She decided that he had the habit of sleep-walking, and had entered her house through a door or window accidentally left open or unlatched. Should she sound the bell for the servants and reveal his presence to the household?

The situation would be called compromising by any gossips anxious to put evil constructions upon the incident, yet the fact of summoning the servants would prove that there had been no secrecy or subterfuge, and she made her decision.

It was only a step to the bell-cord. Reaching it, she gave a pull that roused a bell with a loud jingle in a remote part of the mansion. Feet were soon heard pattering outside, and the servants entered with lights, but the stranger had disappeared. No trace was found of him, high or low, and no bolt, clasp, or lock had been tampered with.

In the morning the woman called on her cousin and related her adventure, describing the man with some minuteness. The reaction of her hostess was indeed surprising. The cousin fell into a chair and cried out in amazement: "That was Mr. Gamere, the man to whom I am engaged to be married. What on earth was he doing in your bedroom?"

Both women agreed it was something which could not be explained.

Before the week came to an end, a message arrived from the waterfront. A ship had docked from London with the body of Mr. Gamere aboard. He had died at sea at the very hour when his apparition was seen in the bedroom.

A weird tale of the cemetery strangely similar to that of

Mrs. Copeland * at Sable Island, Nova Scotia, concerns a lady named Maynadier. She is said to have died suddenly, after which she was quickly buried in the graveyard adjoining the White Marsh Church.

It was then discovered that Mrs. Maynadier had been buried still wearing a large heirloom ring. The story was repeated at the local tavern within hearing of two former occupants of the Annapolis jail, who that very night dug the coffin up, and then attempted in vain to pull the ring off a swollen ring finger.

Finally, to their chagrin, they were forced to cut the finger off in order to get the ring before they fled the area with all haste. Crossing the Bay to Annapolis, the miscreants then disposed of the ring and were never seen in the area again.

Meanwhile, Mrs. Maynadier, whose husband in 1711 was rector of the church, actually had not been dead at all, but merely in a cataleptic fit. She recovered consciousness after the criminals cut off her finger, and stumbled and crawled to the rectory where her bereaved husband was being comforted. Falling in a faint before him, the lady was soon put to bed and given treatment. It is said that she recovered entirely and lived many years more.

Another story concerns the famous painter, Charles Peale, who was commissioned to paint the portrait of three beautiful daughters, members of the Tilghman family. They were living in Talbot County, Maryland, at their ancestral home near St. Michaels.

One of the daughters, Mary, fell in love with Peale, but her father refused permission for their marriage.

Not allowed to see Mary again, Peale finished her por-

---

* Mrs. Copeland, sole shipwreck survivor, was choked to death before her index finger was removed so that a wrecker on the island could obtain the ring.

trait from memory, and it is said to have the best resemblance of all three. Her ghost is often seen searching for her lost lover. Before the turn of the present century, a coach-and-four was occasionally observed as it would sweep into the Tilghman driveway, wait a reasonable length of time, and then drive off into the night without a passenger.

Incidentally, General Lloyd Tilghman of Civil War fame was a prisoner of war at Fort Warren, Boston Harbor, in 1863.

Across the Bay from Annapolis near Easton, Maryland, the Old White Marsh Church was built in 1658. One wall of the church still stands. The ancient cemetery there is said to be regularly haunted by the ghost of a man killed by mistake in Revolutionary days. The cemetery is famous for being the final resting place of Robert Morris, father of the great financial genius of the American Revolution.

The Governor William Paca House on Prince George Street in Annapolis is now being restored by the Historic Annapolis group. Possibly the renovation has upset the ghosts and they have decided that nocturnal strolls will relax their spiritual beings. A few months ago not one but two Annapolis guards assigned to protect state properties suddenly left their jobs. By means of a "confidential grapevine" it has been learned that the reason for the guards resigning was that they had been stationed relatively close to the Paca House. On several occasions the two men were startled to see "a gentleman in colonial dress passing by the lighted windows of the second floor of the Paca House."

Governor Paca, one of the signers of the Declaration of Independence, had a daughter of outstanding beauty. When she fell in love with a commoner, the Governor forbade their marriage, and the young man went away. In similar fashion to the Waving Girl of Elba Island,

Georgia,* the Paca girl waited in vain for him, pining away year after year. Her love, however, went beyond the mortal world, and long after her death she was seen descending the grand staircase to the main floor of the Paca House.

When she reached the lower steps, it was customary for her to raise her hands and walk across to the other side of the room where she would meet a young man in gray. They would stand facing each other for a few moments, after which she would return up the staircase. The young man in gray would then heave a sigh, walk toward the front door, but then dissolve completely into nothingness.

In 1940 a wing of the Brice House in Annapolis was in need of repairs. When the plaster was taken off in one room, a closet door no one knew about was revealed. Chipping away the mortar, the workmen then cleared the area around the forgotten door. When they pried it open, the skeleton of a woman faced them. †

According to Gary Hogan, writing in the *Chesapeake Bay Magazine* for July 1971, one of the Brice family had been concealed in the room with the closet because she was insane and the family did not want to take her to an asylum. When she died, to avoid legal complications her remains were placed in the closet. The room was redone after they sealed the door, as they thought, forever.

---

* A Miss Florence Martus, daughter of the keeper of a lighthouse near Fort Pulaski, was engaged to a sailor who never returned. Day after day, year after year, she waved to every ship coming into the harbor, hoping that he would be coming back to her. He never did.

† The tale is somewhat similar to that of Castle Island in Boston Harbor, later used by Edgar Allan Poe in his masterful *Cask of Amontillado*.

V

⚓

Burr's House of Misfortune

Charles Montgomery Skinner was one of the great research writers on the subject of ghosts at the turn of the century. An associate editor of the Brooklyn *Eagle,* Skinner journeyed all over the American continent whenever he heard of an apparition about which he might write.

Reaching Cranberry, New Jersey, one day in 1901, Skinner went at once to a pre-Revolutionary house often associated with the names of Washington, Lafayette, Jefferson, and Hamilton. It is believed that had these been the only guests at the mansion, a ghost would never have appeared there.

Standing at the corner of the New Brunswick pike and King George's highway, the old coach road from New York to Philadelphia, this colonial mansion was a fine old place already when it was bought by Commodore Thomas Truxton, the famed privateer of the United States Navy.

To Truxton's eventual unhappiness, he knew Aaron Burr, the "brilliant, persuasive, handsome, ambitious, unprincipled schemer." Burr was an athlete, a dead shot, a man of reading, a skilled debater, and a clever politician. His power over women was remarkable, and scores of them suffered dishonor from their confidence in his promises.

In 1804, when he suffered a political setback, Burr picked a quarrel with Alexander Hamilton, Secretary of the Treasury, and challenged him to a duel. The two men had been fellow students at Princeton. Burr charged Hamilton with being the cause of his defeat for the Presidency, a post won by Jefferson.

Hamilton did not believe in dueling. Nevertheless, fearing to be posted as a coward and used as an example of cowardice if he refused, he accepted the challenge and went calmly to his death on the Weehawken Palisades. He fired into the air, and then Burr deliberately shot him to death.

The disgraced survivor of this affair fled to Cranberry and was reluctantly allowed by Thomas Truxton to occupy a room on the top floor of the mansion. The room was reached by an ingenious secret stair behind the fireplace, which had been constructed when the scene of Revolutionary activities shifted to New Jersey.

At an early opportunity Burr fled the country. After attempting to found a rival republic in the West and to liberate Mexico from the Spaniards, he stood trial for treason. Later he died in poverty and neglect.

The gloomy, wicked spirit of the man had no other home, so it apparently encamped as a ghost in the place where it had been received in partial friendship. Ill luck then fell on nearly all who had to do with the place. Truxton engaged in speculations, lost his money, and moved away.

A judge whose severities won general dread and hate succeeded Truxton. The official endured the pressure of public opinion to such a degree that the place was no longer a happy home. Residence in the house seemed to coarsen and brutalize him, and he imposed the law to the letter, once sentencing a man to death for stealing a piece of cloth.*

An elderly Quaker, who next bought the house, was married to a young wife who presently became a slave to opium. He shut her up in Burr's room, but she lowered a basket of money to passing schoolchildren so they could buy the drug for her. How much the ghost of Burr should be blamed for her addiction to opium is a question still debated in New Jersey.

A servant, detected in smuggling pills to her chamber, was beaten senseless and locked in the cellar on a bread-and-water diet for a month. Shortly afterward the woman killed herself. The Quaker had another trouble in the form of a son who had inherited no Quaker instincts of peace or propriety, but had become wild, brawling, drunken, and unruly. He had ridden a pair of horses through the streets, standing on their backs like a circus performer and lighting cigars with ten-dollar bills. He had ridden the horses into a pond, where they drowned. Soon afterward, he tumbled over the banister on the third story and was killed, his blood leaving a stain on the floor that was still to be seen at the turn of the century. Finally the Quaker lost his fortune and disappeared.

Next came a slave-owner from the South, with some of his slaves. The servants burned his barns and ran away, or died on his hands, one of them falling dead before the fire while fiddling for a dance. This owner, too, lost money and moved. A retired army officer who followed him suffered bankruptcy within a year.

---

* Rachel Wall, of Boston's Long Wharf fame, was executed for robbing a woman of her hat!

The next occupant of the house of misfortune was a physician, who thereafter lost heavily from barn burners and poisoners of cattle, though his wife had placed crosses and horseshoes above all the doors and windows.

Then followed a financier, who lost his fortune and political prestige, and his wife her reason and her life. Last in the line was a distiller, who came to his end by a hemorrhage, his wife dying in the same manner.

Now and then there were whispers of footfalls in the passage leading to Burr's chamber, and of shadows on the walls cast by no living being. Nevertheless, Aaron Burr, the evil genius of the house, worked more commonly in silence and in secret, if we are to believe stories that have been told in the last few years.

VI

⚓

Ghosts at Minot's Light

Minot's Light has always been a favorite location to visit when there is time enough. It is a relatively long trip by water from Boston to that sixth "wonder of the world" not too far out to sea from Cohasset and Scituate.

Erected because of scores of shipwrecks in the area, the first Minot's Light was illuminated initially on January 1, 1850. On April 17, 1851, the flimsy tower fell into the sea with the loss of both keepers.

A new tower was finished in 1860 and lighted for the first time on November 15 of that year. Its famed one-four-three code spelling out *I Love You* still flashes in the year 1972, but its power has been dimmed. The ladder has been removed where it entered the water so that to climb Minot's Light today is a problem.

Every important location up and down this romantic coastline has its legends and ghost stories, and Minot's Ledge Light is no exception. Some of the stories about this lighthouse may be more than mere legends, but because of the difficulty of placing time and persons they cannot receive the stamp of absolute fact.

The first story is about the work at the tower. Since cleaning the lens and the lamp is an integral part of the job at a lighthouse, anything out of the ordinary about this duty is likely to attract attention. One morning, a short time after the Civil War, the head keeper at Minot's Light suddenly realized that something strange had happened. The lamp and the lens had been brightly polished that morning, although the assistant keeper, whose task it was to shine them, was still asleep. When it was time to awaken his helper, the head keeper asked him about the cleaning of the lamp and lens. The assistant was as surprised as his superior to learn that the work had already been done. The following week it was the assistant's turn to notice that the same procedure had been repeated, although neither man had performed the task. There may be another explanation, but the ghosts of two keepers lost when the old lighthouse crashed into the sea received full credit for the polishing of the lens and lamp of Minot's Ledge Light.

For many years mariners sailing past the lighthouse have been insisting that they hear strange voices and see ghostlike figures clinging to the lower section of the ladder. It is said that Portuguese fishermen who usually took their compatriot Joseph Antoine out to the Light to serve his turn as keeper, in later years saw the ghost of their friend many times while passing the Rock. This belief became so strong that, according to Keeper Fitzpatrick, many Portuguese fishermen do not dare to venture close to the new stone tower today. It is said that the ghost of young Antoine has usually been heard and seen just prior to northeast storms when the specter puts in an appearance apparently to warn his countrymen away from the dangers of the ledge. Many sailors of a former generation are said to have heard his shrill, high-pitched tones, and to have seen him grasping the lower rungs of the lighthouse ladder, with the gathering surf sweeping over him, as he cried out, "Keep away, keep away."

There are those who tell of the lighthouse keeper at the Rock who was a good workman and who enjoyed his position, until one day an obsession seized him. It is an absurd thought, but he was dissatisfied that there were no normal square corners in the lighthouse. The idea dwelt in his mind till at last he could stand it no longer. This individual, who until then had been perfectly content at the tower, gradually went from bad to worse. Finally, he was compelled to resign his post at this great American beacon, simply because he became obsessed with the ridiculous idea that there were no square corners at the lighthouse.

Another story concerns the strange tapping at the tower. In the former lighthouse it was the custom of the head keeper to signal to his assistant by rapping on the stovepipe that went up through the various floors, in order to inform him that the watch was over. The assistant would rap back to reply that he was coming. But in the new lighthouse an electric bell was installed to call the assistant. One night, however, something happened that has never been satisfactorily explained.

As the midnight watch was drawing to a close, the head keeper was sitting in the watchroom, thinking of the destruction of the old tower. When he was about to get up, he leaned forward and tapped his pipe against the table. A few moments later he was amazed to hear an answering tap from below, although the only other living person at the Light was fast asleep.

Nonplussed as to what to do, he decided to wait for a few minutes. Then he tapped again, and once more from the depths of the granite structure came the answering tap.

He hazarded the guess that the assistant was awake, and perhaps getting dressed, so he waited, in fact he waited for some time, yet nobody appeared. Finally he rang the bell, the usual signal, and after a short wait received the usual reply from below. The steps of the keeper's helper were soon heard on the iron stairs, and when the assistant finally appeared his superior recounted the weird incident. Needless to say, both men were quite startled, especially when they recalled that a tapping from below had been the signal in the old tower where the two men had perished in the great gale.

The story has persisted through the years that the reason for the removal of the famous Longfellow's Chair from its position of active service in front of the tower to a place of honor it later occupied near the bell on the lower parapet, was the death of a lady who fell into the sea. She was being hoisted up to the landing in the chair when suddenly a great wave startled those in the boat below, causing them to release the guide rope. The chair banged against the tower halfway up, and the lady fell out and was killed. I mention this story only because it has been told and is still being told, although the episode does not seem to have any foundation in fact.

A head keeper of Minot's Light once remarked, "The trouble with our life here is that we have too much time to think." Rumor has it that around fifty years ago a new assistant keeper thought too much and decided to cut his throat with a razor. Unfortunately he bled to death before the head keeper discovered him.

Another story purporting to be true, concerns the assitant keeper who was working one day on the davits holding the lighthouse boat. He stood in the boat and let himself down over the side when suddenly there was a crack, and the woodwork in the bow of the dory gave way. Down fell the keeper while the boat hung by the stern. Although he struck the water below with great force he was not seriously injured. The suggestion was put forward at the time that the dory had been weakened by someone anxious to obtain a position at the tower should a vacancy occur.

In 1935 Larry McDavitt of the Boston *American* took one of the most unusual pictures ever taken of Minot's Light. Rowed out to the vicinity of the ledge in a boat after a heavy storm, McDavitt "caught" a high wave as it beat against the tower fully fifty feet in the air. The picture was published many times, but the photographer never received the credit due him.

There are several incidents concerning Minot's Light with which the writer has had a more or less personal connection, including a dive he made a few years ago from the top of the ladder at the lighthouse into the water. The height was not so great as professionals attempt, but because of the element of danger associated with the ledge, the newspapers gave more attention to the incident than it deserved.

On November 15, 1935, the seventy-fifth anniversary of the first illumination of Minot's Light, the writer and his wife were part of a group that flew over the tower from Boston.* As the plane roared over the top of the tower, Mrs. Snow scattered flowers upon the waters where Joseph Wilson and Joseph Antoine kept their last faithful watch more than eighty years before. As he circled over the Light for the last time, the pilot brought his plane within forty feet of the lightning-rod spindle, and the writer "bombed"

* Among the group were Thomas Johnson of Providence, Rhode Island; Charles W. Gammons, representing the town of Cohasset; George P. Tilton of the Boston Port Authority; Captain George Eaton, Superintendent of the Second District, U.S. Lighthouse Service; Edwin Thompson Ramsdell, photographer; Channing Howard, Winthrop historian; and Dr. William Flynn of Dorchester. The pilot was Captain William H. Wincapaw.

the tower with two packages tied together with a thirty-foot cord. As the bundles fell, the line wrapped itself around the parapet, and the two packages were quickly hauled up by the keepers. One bundle contained a birthday cake for the Light itself, and the other package a book written by the author about the lighthouse.

Perhaps the greatest thrill the writer ever experienced in connection with Minot's Light was on November 26, 1939. For several years before this, we had made futile attempts to take airplane pictures of the waves as they ran up the granite sides of the tower after a great storm. Because of the speed of the airplane and the infrequent surges of the sea we were always too far away when a wave submerged the tower. On this occasion a northeast gale had swept the coast the previous day, and shortly before noon that Sunday we took off from the East Boston Airport with Pilot Al Leckchied. Others in the plane were Donald Snow and Charles Wyke. When we reached the vicinity of the lighthouse, the seas were intense in their fury, surpassing the descriptions of many writers who have visited Minot's Light. As we reached the lighthouse itself, a great wave threw itself against the impregnable granite structure, surging up to the highest window under the turret. Another curled around the base of the tower, wrapping it in foam, while still another completely hid the lighthouse from view with a curtain of spray. We circled many times snapping picture after picture, wave afer wave. Then, just as we started for home, we noticed a dragger in distress drifting toward the Light. Helpless to aid the ship, we watched with relief while another dragger turned in toward the lighthouse and threw a line to the imperiled men on the drifting craft. The wind blew the line out of reach of the crew. Finally, on the third attempt, the line was made fast, and the tow to Boston began. To this day we have heard no mention of this heroic effort, as those concerned evidently wished to avoid publicity. It was another unsung deed of heroism at sea. But we in the plane had watched the rescue and believe that the men in the second dragger should receive some acknowledgment for this brave act.

VII

Hawkington's Ghost

Francis Haskell was the president of the Massachusetts Marine Historical League for several terms prior to his death some years ago. When his effects were examined after his death, a large bundle of material arrived at my residence in Marshfield, as his last wish was that I be given a chance to examine it.

Among the tales Mr. Haskell had saved from many sources was a weird account concerning a ghost aboard ship. The story source was a page identified only as AND ADVENTURES AT SEA, with the number of the page given as 557.

The story begins when the carpenter of the ship, old Hawkington, fell sick one day and, after a short illness, died. Let us go on with the account:

"He was a man very much respected on board, and everyone was sorry for him. The ship was ordered into port, where they expected to arrive in a few days, so that he might be buried ashore; and a sentry was placed, as usual, in the cockpit.

"The old gentleman had been dead for three or four days, I do not rightly remember which; but as contrary winds had kept us out longer than we expected, it was decided that he should be committed to the deep on the following day. It was decided that I be sentry over the dead body the night before it was to happen.

"My lantern was hanging to a beam, through the discoloured horn of which, a purser's dip was throwing a very poor light, and I stopped to endeavor to improve it by snuffing, or lighting a new candle as might be necessary.

"While I was thus employed, not having finished my job, the door of the dead man's cabin was thrown back with a loud bang, which could only have been effected by a very powerful slam, and I distinctly heard a gruff, hollow voice roar out, 'Give us a light, sentry!'

"The horrid voice and the noise so startled me that I clutched hold of the lantern so hard that the nail on which it had been hanging came out, and the lantern fell to the deck and went out.

"In the darkness I ran for the cockpit ladder, and mounted it. Then several heavy footsteps approached the bottom of the cockpit ladder, and I made my way out on the lower deck.

"I gathered courage enough to look behind me, and there was the ghost of the carpenter slowly climbing the cockpit ladder. Reaching the top step, he rose in what apparently was ominous fashion from out of the cockpit and strode after me.

"I walked faster, but so did the ghost of Mr. Hawkington. I then went up the fore ladder and the ghost followed me. Therefore, I went aft, and it seemed as though I had doubled on the apparition, for I saw it go up the ladder onto the forecastle, where the men on the forecastle soon noticed it.

"The weather was warm. The members of the watch on deck were lying about the forecastle and gangways, some asleep and others looking at the moon which was then shining as bright as could be.

"The ghost appeared to take no notice of any of them, but followed the path of the walk the old gentleman, Mr. Hawkington, was accustomed to take when alive. He still kept his hands behind him, and his chin on his breast, as if he were in deep thought.

"Presently one of the men made him out. He roused his nearest watchmate, pointing out the ghost to him.

" 'I say, Tom, I'm blest if that ain't the old carpenter! Here he comes, and I shall be off.' The speaker arose quickly and walked aft. The whisper went the rounds rapidly, and in a few minutes the forecastle was as clear as if it had been raining. The ghost now had the area all to himself.

"The men crowded aft to the quarterdeck.

" 'What do you men want here?' asked the officer of the watch.

"No one was anxious to answer the question at first, but finally when it was repeated, the captain of the forecastle replied. He was a sturdy old tar, and muttered something about the carpenter's ghost. He often had stated that he would sooner be the devil himself at anytime than his ghost.

"The officer shouted back at him, 'What's that you say, that you saw the carpenter's ghost?'

"A dozen sailors then called out, 'The carpenter's ghost, the carpenter's ghost!'

" 'What about the carpenter's ghost?' came the officer's question. 'Be off forward, you blockheads, and don't be stopping up the gangway in this manner.'

" 'He is walking the forecastle!' came the answer from a dozen throats.

" 'Nonsense, men, nonsense. Mr. Hawkington's dead, and I am astonished at you.'

" 'He is walking the forecastle right now,' came the answer, 'and he is wearing the very same hat I covered for him, and the same monkey jacket, and the end of his chalk line is hanging from his pocket.'

" 'Go forward, sir, and see for yourself.'

" 'Parcel of fools,' exploded the lieutenant. 'Make a lane there and let me go forward.' A lane speedily opened up, and the lieutenant boldly walked forward, until he reached the bow of the barge, and then he stopped.

"There was the apparition, walking back and forth, just as the men had claimed, and the lieutenant's courage began to fail him. He then decided that it was not prudent to approach any closer, and shouted out.

" 'Mister Hawkington, is that you?'

" 'Sir,' came the answer from the supposed apparition.

"The lieutenant decided that it was then a good time to report the incident to the captain. Knocking on the captain's door, for the master was then asleep, the lieutenant called out that the carpenter was walking the deck.

" 'Well, sir,' exclaimed the captain, awakening.

" 'The carpenter is on the forecastle,' explained the lieutenant again.

" 'Let him be on the forecastle, and be damned,' concluded the captain, and rolled over to resume his slumbers.

"Evidently the carpenter had suffered a trance, and actually came out of the trance while in the cockpit awaiting to be thrown or cast into the sea.

"When questioned later, all the carpenter could remember was that he heard two bells strike, and he thought that it was the morning watch, and time to turn out, and so he roused out, called for a light as usual, fumbled about and found his clothes, and giving a curse or two to me for putting out the light, bundled on deck as was his custom."

VIII

The Children's Ghosts

Besides the New Haven storm-ship and the well-known "Flying Dutchman," certain other shadow-craft sail in American waters, and the ghosts of sailors fly across the seas in the guise of petrels, or Mother Carey's chickens, enduring purgatory and doomed never to find rest till their sins are forgiven.

Among the phantom ships that may be met, now and again, is the Spanish treasure-galleon aboard of which Captain Don Sandovate was killed by his mutinous sailors. As he was dying he begged the men for water, and they jeered and held the precious liquid just beyond his reach. For this they are condemned to roam the Atlantic until doomsday, suffering eternally from thirst. You will know the ship well enough, if you meet her, for a crew of skeletons will hail you as you pass, and cry for water till you are out of hearing.*

In the seventeenth century another vessel had freighted

---

* For another skeleton crew, see my *Great Atlantic Adventures*, p. 250.

at Salem, Massachusetts, for England. All was ready for her departure, the passengers were on board, and the crew were about to cast off, when a young man and woman, richly dressed, handsome, and of distinguished bearing, hurried down the wharf and asked to be taken to England. They had money and they wanted a cabin. None had ever seen them before. During the few minutes spent in talk upon this request the wind went about and blew dead ahead, so that the sailors began to feel apprehensive, and were heard grumbling about taking people on that trip who might bring bad luck to the vessel. The master yielded to the plea of the young couple, however, and on Friday, the wind being favorable once more, he set sail for the old country. The vessel never reached England. It is thought that she went down in Massachusetts Bay, for there are those who see her occasionally as they sail between Cape Ann and Cape Cod. Her hull shines in the dark, she rides through the air a foot above the water, and a row of white faces can be seen staring over the side.

Still another story concerns an ancient hulk that had lain at a wharf in a Maine port, her years of usefulness ended. Youngsters scrambled over her and played tag on her decks and hide-and-seek in her hold and cabins. They pretended to steer her by the venerable old wheel on all sorts of voyages—to the island where Crusoe lived and to the lands of Ali Baba and Lilliput.

One summer afternoon thirteen boys and girls were playing aboard the craft. Suddenly the rotten cable parted and the old ship, whose forefoot everyone supposed had grounded in half a fathom of mud, moved slowly out on the tide. At first the children cheered and laughed to feel the old hull in motion, but as the distance from the land grew wider they saw their danger and began to call. Several fishermen ran to the water and set their sails to the wind—in vain, for a chill gale had sprung up; then a fog covered the whitening sea, and mercifully hid the tragedy. This was many years ago, but even today, on occasion, a moldy shape goes by, lighted by the moon. Faint, pathetic little voices call, asking that a company of children be allowed to go ashore and visit their homes and loved ones once more.

IX

A Ghost's Search

To those who spend vacations at Freeport in the Bahamas, Great Isaac Cay is well known. My first view of the Great Isaac Light was thirty years ago. Flying some sixty miles off the coast of Florida, suddenly I saw it off to the left, about forty miles distant. It was an inspiring sight, with its fifteen brilliant horizontal bands of red and white. Since that day I have been interested in the cay on which the light stands.

Some years before the lighthouse was erected on Great Isaac Island, a terrible hurricane visited the Bahamas, leaving in its wake countless shipwrecks and innumerable personal tragedies. When the storm subsided, wreckers and salvagers from nearby Bimini went out on their usual tours of the various cays. Two brothers, who had been sailing around the vicinity all that day, were returning home by the light of a rising moon which had just managed to break through the threatening clouds.

Suddenly, as they were passing Great Isaac Cay, the

wrecker at the wheel, Ralph, turned to his brother with a horrified expression.

"George," he stammered, "did you hear that awful scream?"

George, who was slightly deaf but would not admit it, told him to get back to the wheel and forget any noises that he might hear.

Again came the awful, piercing scream of a being in distress. The sound was inhuman in its eeriness. Ralph looked over toward the island, now covered with light from the moon. There on the rocky shore he could make out what seemed to be a large white horse.

"George," continued the man at the wheel, "I can't stand it. Let's go ashore and find out what it is. If we don't it will haunt me all my life. Now, come on, I mean it!"

"All right," George reluctantly consented. "Let's try to get ashore, but remember where the little inlet is, and don't miss it."

Half an hour later the two Bimini wreckers had landed on Great Isaac Cay and were making their way laboriously over the giant boulders. Again and again the screams echoed from the other side of the island. When the brothers finally climbed over the ledges and reached the rocky shore, there was nothing in sight. Hurrying down to the water's edge, George located the object of his search—a beautiful white horse, lying dead between two jagged rocks. What he had heard had been the final death throes of the injured animal. Evidently the hurricane had destroyed a vessel on which the horse had been part of the cargo, and the poor, frightened beast had swum to the cay and fatally injured himself attempting to get ashore there.

"I wonder what ship that horse came from?" Ralph remarked, but George had had enough.

"Now, let's forget the whole thing and get back to Bimini."

Ralph agreed to leave but asked George if he minded walking back the other way to the boat. As they went around the other side of the island, they discovered the fragments of a wrecked ship strewn up and down the shore. Scores of human bodies littered the beach at that point. Then Ralph made his discovery.

"Look, George, look there," and on the sand they both saw a woman with a baby in her arms. Bending over her, they realized that she was dead. But the baby had survived the two days that had elapsed since the hurricane. Some strange, mysterious force had allowed the child to live while all others from the ship had died.

The two men then tried to remove the infant from the death clutch of the mother. Finally, they had to slip the baby out of its garments to release it. Wrapping the child in their own clothing, they turned away, leaving the body of the woman alone on the shore, her fingers still clutching the baby's clothing.

Arriving home, they moored the boat and rowed ashore as fast as they could. George ran ahead to waken his mother while Ralph came more slowly with the child. Their mother came to the door of her bedroom, drawing her robe about her, and they placed the orphaned child in her arms. Amazed as she was, the mother still realized that the infant required immediate care. When the baby was fed and clothed, the boys sat down and told their story. Finally, the baby was adopted and lived at Bimini for several years.

A few years after this episode, the British Government sent a vessel to Great Isaac Cay with the parts of the dismantled Great Isaac Light aboard. Beacons, in those days, were generally made in England and shipped all over the world. A gang of workers brought the pieces ashore and set them up. Several months later when the tall lighthouse was nearly completed, a workman was standing on the rocky beach when he noticed what appeared to be a woman furtively making her way along the cay. She was evidently seaching for something. From time to time she uttered a low moan, and then spoke in a low, faltering voice, "My baby, my baby!"

Rushing into the bunkhouse where his companions were assembled, the workman told them what he had seen and heard. Laughter and ridicule met his words. The laughter didn't last long, however. Soon afterward the foreman of the construction gang walked down to the water's edge to watch the beautiful sight of a full-rigged sailing ship passing the island in the rays of the rising moon. When the ship had disappeared in the distance, he started back toward his quarters. He was amazed to see a woman walking in a furtive manner, repeating a moaning cry, "My baby, my baby!" From that night until the lighthouse was completed on August 1, 1859, the Phantom Lady of Great Isaac was seen by one workman after another. With the lighthouse completed, the working gang left the island, but not before they had warned the keepers about the Phantom Lady.

Almost every year from 1859 until 1913 the Phantom Lady of Great Isaac put in an appearance. Many of the keepers have told stories of their adventures with the Lady. Usually they saw her searching the shore where the child had been found in her arms at the time of the hurricane. Almost invariably her appearance was accompanied by a rising moon.

In the year 1913, however, the keeper reported that she attempted a new venture—climbing the lighthouse steps. One night, as he was descending the spiral staircase of the tower, he saw a form below slowly ascending toward him. It was the Phantom Lady climbing the lighthouse stairs, and he needed to pass her on the stairs in order to escape. Finally the Lady of Great Isaac was only two turns of the spiral stairs below him—her hooded head bent forward as she drew closer. Her soft, plaintive voice was quite distinct to the terrorized keeper. He heard her utter plainly the words, "My baby, my baby!" The keeper was petrified with fear and was unable to move up or down. The woman came still closer until she was only one complete turn of the spiral staircase away from him. Summoning all his courage and strength, he forced himself to turn and run up the steps into the turret, slam the trap door, and place a heavy crate of machinery over it. There he stood, shivering and apprehensive, until the first gray glow of dawn assured him that he could put out the light and descend to the rocky ledge below. But, poor man, he waited an extra hour after the sun came up; he had not the slightest wish to meet the Phantom Lady of Great Isaac again.

The keeper asked for and received permission to transfer to another lighthouse. The new keeper, arriving in 1914, was determined to rid the island of the phantom once and for all. The following day he held a committal service at dusk on the very part of the cay where he had been told the bodies were washed ashore years before. His sincere religious bearing and his tone of humility impressed all who were present at the service, and the entire atmosphere of the island seemed more livable almost immediately after the ceremony ended.

Since that service at Great Isaac Cay, the Phantom Lady has never reappeared. There are those who claimed that the Lady was the spiritual form of the drowned mother, seeking her child in death. But because the baby was alive and the mother could not find it in her world, she came back to the cay and searched year after year. After the committal service, the mother abandoned her hopeless quest. That, at least, is the way they tell the story over Bimini way.

X

⚓

The Phantom Aboard the Usk

A resident of Winthrop, Massachusetts, who was born in Wales, one day took me aside to ask if I believed in the existence of ghosts. I told him I was openminded about ghosts in general, and admitted I believed many ghost stories were founded in fact, but in other cases I was sure that the tales were not supernatural in origin.

Eventually my friend left a manuscript with me concerning a phantom aboard the *Usk,* and I include it in this chapter.

"One cloudy day during the height of the American Civil War, a sea captain from Cardiff, Wales, was sailing along the Atlantic Coast of South America heading toward Huacho, a seaport near Lima, Peru. Captain Richard Brown had left Cardiff in his splendid ship, the *Usk,* and at first was hopeful of making a good passage. Encountering bad weather and adverse winds, he lost several weeks' time, but now he was approaching Cape Horn with a fair chance of making up some of his passage schedule. Standing on the quarterdeck, Captain Brown looked out over the waves and wondered how much longer his voyage would last. His answer came to him in a very strange manner.

"Among the shrouds there materialized the beautiful phantom-like vision of a woman clothed in pure white veils. She beckoned Brown to come closer, and the captain eagerly strode across the deck to meet her. She came down and stood beside him, the veils playing around her graceful form.

" 'Go back to the port from which you came,' she told him in a firm unwavering voice. 'Waste no time, but turn your ship back toward Cardiff before you lose her and yourself as well! Tell them that I have so ordained it.'

"With a momentary smile, the vision faded away before his astonished gaze, leaving him alone on the quarterdeck. Shortly afterward a dense fog swept in from the sea and enveloped the ship. Captain Brown regarded the fog as a warning. He retired to his cabin and sent for the first mate and two of the sailors.

" 'Mr. Edwards,' Captain Brown said to the first mate, 'according to my reckonings, we are now some four hundred miles from Cape Horn. Take a look and see if you agree with my location.'

"Edwards stepped forward and examined the chart, rather perplexed at the interview.

" 'Yes, sir,' he replied, 'I agree.'

" 'Well, we are changing our course at once. The new course is northeast, and we are heading back to Cardiff. Furthermore, I do not wish any comments at this time on my plans.'

" 'But, sir, what is wrong? Why are we changing our course, and why are we returning home after all these weeks at sea?'

" 'I think that I made it quite clear, Mr. Edwards, that I would tolerate no questions. I have been given instructions to return at once. My reasons shall, of course, be announced to the owners upon my arrival at Cardiff.' The captain stood up and filled his pipe. As far as he was concerned, the interview was over. But the mate could not understand what had happened to his superior officer and made a final effort to speak.

" 'Captain Brown, what can we possibly tell the owners which will justify such a strange procedure? They'll make trouble for us. We'll be the laughingstock of the waterfront.'

" 'Mr. Edwards,' cried the overwrought captain, 'are you going to carry out my instructions or not?'

" 'Please, sir, I know that you are in command. I fully realize that, sir. But think of what you are asking, and please be reasonable. We both know that no one will believe that you obtained orders here on the South Atlantic. Please, sir, reconsider!'

" 'Enough of that!' shouted the captain, and ordered the seamen to step forward. 'Seize Mr. Edwards and place him in irons at once!' The order was quickly carried out, and the captain strode aft to the man at the wheel.

" 'Until further orders the new course is northeast. We are coming about and sailing back to Cardiff.'

"Half an hour later all was quiet aboard the *Usk*. The ship had reversed her course and started on the long weary journey back to the British Isles. Word had been circulated about the ship that Captain Brown had received orders to return to Wales from a phantom. The *Usk* made good time on the return voyage and a month and a half later was sailing up the British Channel. Entering the port of Cardiff, Captain Brown warped his ship into the dock and went up to the shipping offices as soon as possible. There he explained to the representatives of his firm the extraordinary event that had caused him to return to port.

"The owners were outraged and called the authorities. They asked that Captain Brown be imprisoned at once for his strange act. He had been absent from Cardiff for five months and had sailed almost to Cape Horn and back without visiting a single port. Expenses for food, clothing, and wages were heavy, and the voyage had been a failure. The cargo of coal and iron was still aboard.

"A hearing was held during which the mate, Edwards, gave his story. Several of the sailors also testified. At the end of the hearing the captain's papers were taken away from him, and he was declared unfit to be in command of a ship. Captain Brown was dishonored and ridiculed.

"A week later another captain accepted a commssion to sail the *Usk* to the Peruvian port of Huacho, but, for some inexplicable reason, he had difficulty in assembling a full crew. Word of the last purposeless voyage had spread around the waterfront. The phantom of the Atlantic was so vividly described by the former members of the *Usk*'s crew, none of whom had seen her, that for many days other superstitious Welsh sailors shunned the mystery ship. Eventually, however, the crew was made up, and the *Usk* sailed once more from Cardiff, bound again for Huacho on the western coast of South America.

"When the *Usk* again sailed out into the Bristol Channel, her owners returned to their counting offices relieved that the voyage had actually begun. Four months later they received a dispatch from Coquimbo, Chile, saying that the *Usk* had been destroyed by fire at sea. Flames had broken out in a storeroom when a candle ignited some material, and the blaze had spread so rapidly that it was impossible to check it.

"But the sailors of Cardiff who had refused to go aboard

the *Usk* had another explanation. They remembered the dishonored captain and the warning he claimed to have received from the phantom. Gathering in little knots and queues on the pier at Cardiff, these men of the sea discussed the loss of the sailing ship *Usk,* agreeing that the vessel had gone down because of the total disregard for the warning of the beautiful phantom."

XI

⚓

The Miracle of Le Bourdais

Grindstone Island, one of the lonely Magdalen group, is fifty-six miles due north of Eastern Point on Prince Edward's Island in Canada. My grandfather Joshua N. Rowe was shipwrecked there in the 1850s as a boy of twelve, and it was there that I was told the most fantastic *true* story I have ever heard.

In the year 1872 a terrible blizzard hit Grindstone Island shortly after church services on Sunday, December 15. The storm continued with such fury that few island inhabitants left their homes for several days. On Thursday, during a lull in the blizzard, three brave lads decided to go down to the beach. Reaching the water's edge, they found the wreckage of a ship scattered up and down the shore at the foot of the cliffs and beyond the high-tide mark.

For several hours the three boys gathered salvage from the wreck. When it grew dark, they lighted flares and began to make their way homeward. As they passed a large mass of wreckage, there emerged from behind it a gigantic creature, seemingly eight feet high and snow white. This

incredible figure advanced on them slowly, uttering gut-
tural, inarticulate noises. Dropping their flares and their
spoils, the boys fled to their homes.

The next morning the storm returned in full force, but
by afternoon conditions were relatively normal. News of
the wreck spread quickly, and about twenty men went
down to the shore where the disaster had taken place. Few
of them had paid any attention to the strange story of the
three boys, dismissing the huge white creature as a large
owl, or, at worst, a polar bear that had come in on an ice
floe.

The men worked all that day at the wreck, which they
found had been loaded with wheat and was named the
Calcutta. They were able to save several tons of wheat but
very little else. However, the spars and rigging, anchors
and chain were located and stored for future use.

When the sun went down the men concluded that the
day had been a profitable one and, lighting flares, began
their homeward journey across the frozen marshes and
fields.

As they passed a haybarn, again without warning, an
enormous white shape eight feet in height reared up at
them from out of the snowdrifts and slowly advanced.
The creature was so frightful that every last man dropped
whatever he was carrying and ran as fast as he could for
home, screaming with terror.

Reaching the village, the men lost no time in calling at
the home of Father Charles Boudreault to tell him of their
fantastic experience. The good Father tried to comfort
them as best he could, but their fear was so deep-seated
and their vision so vivid that the men couldn't forget it.
"All right," Father Boudreault told them. "Tomorrow I
shall accompany you to the scene of your encounter. Now

all of you go home to your good wives and say no more about it."

Early the next morning Father Boudreault appeared in front of the church, and soon a dozen men joined him, each armed with a gun. The others decided to stay at home and protect their wives—or so they claimed.

After an hour's walk the party reached the haybarn, but a light snow the night before had obliterated all evidence of the strange encounter. The men returned to the village and decided to search again after lunch. That afternoon the tide was out, and the group walked along the beach to the scene of the wreck. Afterward they continued across to the haybarn without finding a sign of the huge white creature.

However, as Father Boudreault walked across the meadow in back of the barn, he saw something that excited him. "Come over here!" he called to the others. Soon they were all gathered around him. "Look!" The men glanced down into the snow to discover several impressions of the strangest footprints they had ever seen. The prints were about twenty-two inches long and almost twelve inches wide. What unusual creature could have such a foot?

Father Boudreault followed the tracks for a short distance and soon realized that it was a two-legged something which he was tracking in the snow! But what two-legged animal could this be? And the men had claimed it was eight feet high!

On and on they walked, as the afternoon sun dropped lower and lower in the sky. Father Boudreault continued to walk in front of the others, but they were all on the alert, their guns ready to shoot whatever the thing might be—ghost, giant, or polar bear. "What can it be?" each man said to his neighbor. A polar bear, after all, doesn't walk on its hind legs, nor were there men eight feet tall roaming around the Magdalen Islands.

Then, far in the distance, they saw a huge form, evidently on its side, down on the beach. They approached the gigantic creature slowly with their guns ready for action. By this time the sun had set. As soon as the men lighted their flares, Father Boudreault advanced alone toward the form in the snow. Then he was at the side of the creature. He reached out and touched it. When he told the men that his hand had encountered frozen snow, they were more perplexed than ever, for they doubted that there could be an icy ghost.

Father Boudreault now walked around to the other side of the creature. It was indeed huge, more than nine feet in girth and almost eight feet long.

Still the priest did not know what it could possibly be. Several of the men crowded behind him, and in the light of their flares he could distinguish what appeared to be the head of the creature. And what a head it was—almost four feet wide and three feet long!

"Hold the torches closer," Father Boudreault told the men, and soon there was good illumination by which to examine the creature's head. The priest crouched down on his knees to look more closely, and now he could distinguish two cavities where eyes were located. But the entire body, except for its eyes and mouth, was so covered with ice and snow that it was still impossible to tell what sort of creature it really was.

Then the eyes began to open and close, and a horrible inarticulate moan came, it seemed, from the very depths of the creature's soul. Again and again the weird moan issued forth.

In a moment the huge creature's massive arms, two feet

thick and four feet long, began to move, feebly at first, and then with more strength.

The priest leaned over to see more clearly, and as he did so, his overcoat flew open, revealing his Roman collar and breastpiece, with a silver cross dangling below. The creature now appeared to be considerably excited, and its unhappy moans grew more agitated. Then, as Father Boudreault leaned closer and closer the creature made a final effort, and the priest heard the single word: "Father!"

"Mon Dieu!" shouted the priest. "Incredible as it seems, this creature is a living man. We've got to get him to the nearest house. He's been frozen by the blizzard, and the snow has caked over him until it is actually from one to two feet in thickness. Let's carry him away. Come on, men."

Several of the Canadians went down to the shore, where they found a piece of planking nine feet long and of sufficient width. It took every man present to help carry the huge form back to the village, for the ice and snow made its total weight over a thousand pounds.

That night the men and women of Grindstone Island worked far into the early morning hours, first chopping away the outside ice, and then thawing away that portion nearest the flesh with heavy cold towels. Gradually a human form emerged from within the fantastic shape that had been brought into the house: a man six feet eight in height and weighing, without ice and snow, no less than three hundred and ten pounds! It was his enormous physique that had kept him alive.

Later the man was questioned by Father Boudreault. He was found to be Auguste Le Bourdais, the first mate of the wheat ship *Calcutta* and the only man saved. He could only recall that after the wreck of his ship he had clung a full day and night to a fragment of wreckage in the sea, and that during the days after he reached the shore he had eaten nothing but snow! The sight of Father Boudreault's cross had evidently given him back his senses.

Le Bourdais's sufferings were terrible as his limbs began to thaw. Soon he was wishing that he had died in the wreck. A week after his rescue, the islanders realized that they would have to cut off his badly frozen legs. It took ten men to hold him to the table while the amputations were made. But he lived!

When the ice floes melted at the end of May 1873, Le Bourdais was taken to Quebec for another operation. His legs were further shortened so that he could be fitted to peg legs. He later returned to the Magdalen Islands and eventually founded the government telegraph office there. Even with peg legs, he could stand up against anyone in a fight.

PART II GALES

XII

The Enigma *Capsizes*

John Wallace Spencer, in his extremely interesting book *Limbo of the Lost,* tells of an unexplained power that is present in the world from time to time, a power that can help men in disasters at sea. Beings from flying saucers are often involved for good or bad in this greatest of mysteries. The story that follows may fall into the category of a possible visit by these denizens of space.

One hundred and two years ago the Bath-built schooner *Enigma* sailed away from that Maine City, bound for Charleston, South Carolina. Aboard was young Gilmore Marr of Bath, who was beginning the fulfillment of a wish of many years to go on a long ocean voyage. He was never to complete the trip, for he became involved in a fantastic sea story.

Built in the shipyard of F. O. Morse, the *Enigma* was constructed in such a way that her draft was extremely shallow. She also had a substantial centerboard, thus allowing her to maneuver in both shallow and deep water to fit the occasion.

Her fateful voyage began on October 2, 1865, when she left the piers of Bath heavily loaded with lumber and potatoes. J. T. Morse was sailing as master and part owner.* The crew consisted of Cyrus Morse, Gilmore Marr, Joseph Anderson, and Henry W. Small. Although rough weather was encountered, she reached Charleston on October 13 in the good time of eleven days. Late on October 17 her cargo for Charleston had been discharged and she sailed the following day for Mobile. All went well until the twenty-second, when a sudden terrific gale hit the area and soon became a hurricane.

In spite of the howling wind, high seas, and breaking waves, the *Enigma* was weathering the storm, and everyone aboard felt that she would ride it out without trouble. At the height of the storm the captain sighted land, which he soon recognized as the Abaco Islands in the Bahamas. The *Enigma* was kept on course with a meager amount of sail, and drove ahead hour after hour through the gale.

All that day the storm continued, although by nightfall they were still making good progress. As darkness fell Captain Morse believed that the worst was over—although in fact they were, unsuspectingly, approaching the center of the hurricane, known as the eye, which brought temporarily calm weather.

At ten o'clock all the crew retired below except for Gilmore Marr and Joseph Anderson, then standing watch. As Captain Morse went down into the cabin he expressed a hope that the weather would be better when they awakened. An hour later, Joseph Anderson went below for a drink of water. As he stood in the galley, the captain called across from his bunk, "How are things going?"

---

* The *J. T. Morse*, launched in 1904, was named for James T. Morse, then treasurer of the Eastern Steamship Company.

"About as well as can be expected," came the reply.

Taking a piece of bread, Anderson sat down on the companion hatchway and munched away as though there were nothing to worry about. Captain Morse, now quite sure that the storm had ended, offered up a prayer of thanksgiving to God for their preservation. Then he spoke to Anderson: "Keep a sharp lookout, and the other boys will be ready after an hour's sleep."

Leaning over to pat the captain's dog, Anderson then prepared to go up on deck. He started for the companion hatchway. Suddenly the schooner was seized by an apparently irresistible force. The men never knew what it was, for the only one who could possibly tell what happened on deck of the *Enigma* was Gilmore Marr, and they never saw him again. Actually, the *Enigma* was conquered by an overpowering force, and humanity was helpless.

In a split second the schooner was turned completely over. The captain, Cyrus Morse, and Henry Small were thrown from their bunks almost naked, for they had taken off their wet clothes on retiring. Rushing for the companionway, they attempted to force it open, but the pressure of the water was too great, and they could not move it. As the minutes went by, the schooner gave no indication of righting herself, and the captain, standing knee-deep in water in the pitch blackness, realized the seriousness of their predicament.

Slowly the water began to rise in the capsized cabin. Within a short time it was waist-deep. Terrified in the utter darkness, the men wondered if they would ever see the light of day again. Then they began to think about young Marr topside and they decided that if he were still alive, he was the only one who apparently had a chance of escaping. He could be aboard the load of lumber if it had drifted off the schooner, but of course they had no way of knowing. The dog also had vanished.

As the water crept higher and higher, the air space in the cabin slowly grew smaller. The men clung desperately to whatever they could get a grip on. Now the water began to slosh over them with each surge that ripped through the capsized schooner. Finally the force of a wave changed the angle of the cabin so that it became necessary to clamber to the surface to get a breath of air, for the craft was now rocking back and forth. One minute they were in water over their heads and in the next were less than waist-deep in brine.

In the darkness of the overturned wreck the water slowly gained. Then, in a moment of despair, Captain Morse remembered the hatchet that was kept in the cabin. If only he could find it, perhaps he could smash a hole through the hull and escape to the bilge, after which they might hack their way through the seven-inch-thick bottom. He realized that the air would not last forever.

Filling his lungs, he dove down into a corner of the cabin. He fumbled against the bulkhead, groping in the underwater darkness. Three times he had to come up for air, but finally he closed his fingers over the handle of the hatchet. Swimming back to the surface, he jubilantly announced his find to the others, who by this time had given up hope of surviving.

After estimating where he should start cutting a hole through the partition, Morse told his men to stand back. Then he started hacking away. Suddenly there was a cry of pain.

"You've hit me!" shouted Henry Small. "I'm bleeding badly!"

In the darkness the others helped bandage the wound on

Small's left hand. Five minutes later Small crawled out of the way, still nursing his injury.

The other men took their turns with the captain in the attempt to hack a passage through into the hold, but it was terribly slow progress. Several hundred blows later the axe cut through the cabin bulkhead, and after another half hour the opening was large enough for the men to clamber through. Luckily the potatoes which had filled that section of the hold had been taken ashore at Charleston, and there was substantial room to move about in the capsized *Enigma.*

By now the men were numbed with cold and half-drowned as well. Slowly crawling across to where the lumber was stored, they actually fell asleep on the loose planking. Still prisoners, at least they now would be able to get some rest as they awaited whatever Fate had in store for them.

Later they estimated that they must have fallen asleep about three o'clock in the morning. Slumbering until they were awakened by the light of dawn seeping into the hull, they noticed that while they were asleep wave action around the craft had brought the *Enigma* partially back on her beam ends. For an instant everyone thought she would complete her roll and right herself, but in this they were mistaken.

It was lucky she did not turn upright, for the men would have been crushed to death by the fall of the lumber on which they had slept. What did happen was that the deckload of lumber slid away from her at that moment and the masts also went overboard. Suddenly the four survivors were dazzled with bright sunlight, for one of the hatches broke off underwater, and the reflected light penetrated the gloom of the hold.

For the first time since the capsizing the men were able

to see each other. The seamen noticed that the captain was barefooted, with only his trousers on, and was bleeding from scores of cuts and bruises. Small's cut also still bled from time to time.

Once more the water started to gain rapidly, and the men began to fear that they were sinking. After several moments of anxiety, however, the water diminished to a trickle, for evidently there was still enough lumber to keep the hulk afloat on the surface.

By the position of the schooner, Captain Morse figured that a part of the hull must be above the surface. They considered attempting to swim out under water through the broken hatchway and then clambering up on the bottom, but not one of them had enough nerve or energy to try it. Furthermore, they reasoned, there was no assurance that whoever attempted the swim would be able to hold his breath for the necessary period of time.

Morse decided that if he used the hatchet again in an effort to cut through the bottom, they might reach a position on the hull and could thus signal for help. Trapped as they were in the hold, they would never be able to attract attention.

It was now the morning of Tuesday, October 24, 1865, and they set to work again with the axe. The inside hull planks were of hardwood three inches thick, and the outside bottom planking measured four inches. The men now realized they faced a much more difficult task than they had in breaking through the first opening. In addition, their new position was awkward, for they had to strike almost directly overhead. Nevertheless, Cyrus Morse, the captain, and Anderson worked constantly with the axe, but the injured Small could give no help.

All that afternoon and all night long they took turns with the hatchet, and by Wednesday at dawn they could see light coming through the thinnest part of the timbers. With a hatchet now so blunt that it would not cut, they had to chip the fragments away rather than chop through them. Hour after hour went by in this fashion.

Finally the captain thought he could see the suggestion of strong daylight above him. He broke off a fragment of timber the size of a silver dollar, and all at once, with a fearful whistling sound, the compressed air trapped in the cabin began to escape through the tiny aperture. At the same moment, the men could feel the water climb as the schooner began to settle. For a brief interval they panicked, and the captain knew that he would have to act fast. He tore off his trousers and forced the clothing into the hole, thus preventing further escape of air. The whistling noise stopped, and the water made no more progress.

A council was then held. It was decided that they would not attempt another breakthrough until there was a chance of smashing out a section large enough for them all to scramble through and escape. They began again, cutting and chopping. By the time they believed that they were ready, they had cut out an area twelve inches by twenty inches, in every part of which strong light could be seen on the other side of the thin panel.

An impromptu battering ram was then constructed, made of several pieces of lumber tied together with a coil of rope. Acting on a given signal, they all lifted the ram together and smashed it against the section. The panel gave way at once. The captain, directly below the aperture, was caught in the air pressure forcing its way through the hole. The force lifted him right off his feet and pulled him through the opening, up and onto the capsized bottom of the *Enigma!* A moment later all the compressed air had escaped, but Morse quickly helped the others out of the hold, one by one. Each man, emerging from the relative darkness, scanned the sea around him. There was no sail in sight and no sign of Gilmore Marr. He had vanished—as events later proved, forever. The captain's dog, having survived the ordeal in some mysterious fashion, was found alive on the keel. He barked his approval at sighting the men. The schooner began to settle and quickly sank two feet. The men realized they would have drowned if they had not broken through the bottom all at once and escaped as they did.

It was now Thursday, October 25, and they had been sixty-four hours without food or water. Anderson suggested that the dog be eaten, but the others disagreed. Although they were greatly exhausted, the fresh air revived them, and they continued to search the horizon for the sight of a ship. None appeared.

With night coming, Captain Morse ordered preparations for a scaffolding of some sort to be erected on the capsized bottom as a partial shelter. Several scantlings were secured and the hatchet was used to drive them into the centerboard aperture. A crossbar was then constructed some four feet above the deck, with another raised about three feet higher, to signal passing craft.

Terribly thirsty, the men realized that they would soon die unless they had something to drink. The thought of killing the dog was again reluctantly considered. Finally the captain gave his consent. Anderson plunged his sheath knife into the animal and they all drank the blood. Anderson, who consumed more than the others, soon went out of his mind and had to be lashed to the lower crossbar.

That evening the others slept by fastening themselves to the scantlings with lines so that they would not fall overboard. The next day the sailors built a platform two feet wide above the reach of the sea, on which each man could take turns sleeping. They could also stand here to signal should a sail appear.

By Friday the dog's blood was gone. On Saturday they caught a two-foot shark. A heavy rain set in Sunday night which gave them drinking water. The next day was hot, and by the following night the shark had turned green and slimy, so they agreed to throw it away. A flying fish was caught the next afternoon. Six inches long, it proved a good meal.

On Monday they sighted a ship four miles away, but in spite of frantic waving and signaling they were not seen, and the vessel soon vanished over the horizon. By this time they were suffering terribly. Not only were their throats swollen, but their tongues were black and began to protrude. Masses of sores covered their bodies.

The next day Anderson began to fail, and Captain Morse realized that the man could not live many more days. No sail was sighted from Tuesday to Friday, and by Friday night all thought Anderson would die. But Captain Morse did not abandon hope. As he lay down to rest that night, he felt that rescue must be close and decided to talk to the crew.

"There has been a providential hand in many things since we were overturned. I think that means something more than we have yet experienced—our finding the hatchet, and our getting out of the cabin just in time to escape death from the increasing water that flowed in upon us. There is something greater than life now controlling our destiny.

"Our good success in escaping from the hold where we could have lived but a little longer; the saving of that coil of rope for the battering ram, the very one of all we had on board which we would have chosen for our purpose; that rain also, and that fish—God has not given us all this success to forsake us now. Let us see what tomorrow will bring!"

Surely enough, early the next morning, Saturday, the men were overjoyed to see a sail coming toward them and soon recognized the craft as a brig. When she changed her course and headed directly for them, they realized they had been seen.

It was the British brig *Peerless* on a trip from Philadelphia to Matanzas, Cuba. After some delay, the vessel sent out a boat and took them off. Anderson, then unconscious, had to be carried, and the poor man died less than three hours later.

Aboard the brig the sailors continued to suffer from their long exposure. Their throats were now so swollen that they could hardly accept a drop of liquid. Their bodies looked like skeletons, and their emaciated hands and legs were in shocking condition.

Everything possible was done for them. First they were given warm arrowroot tea, a few drops at a time. Then the amount was increased, after which gruel was served, and eventually more solid food.

It was a miracle that they were alive at all, for while on the *Enigma* from Monday to the following Saturday they had had only a little water and the fish fragments. Nevertheless, in spite of their hardships, they slowly improved.

On reaching Cuba they were taken to Matanzas Hospital, where they made rapid progress and were discharged ten days later. Eventually obtaining passage to New England, they arrived home six weeks later. After a few weeks of recuperation, the captain was given a new bark owned by F. O. Morse and was soon far out on the ocean on another voyage. Such is the way of the sea.

For years afterward, Henry Small worked in the shipyards at Bath, Maine. Stinson Lord, of East Weymouth, told me that he remembered the old man, who usually held his hand in a peculiar way because of the hatchet cut. He said, "We always called him 'Pleasant William' because he was able to swear in such a pleasant, loud, and clear voice that we could hear him half a mile away on a cold, frosty morning."

But no one could explain successfully why the *Enigma* capsized, or how the captain had successfully predicted that the very next day a ship would appear and rescue them.

XIII

The Life-Saving Service

Only one of the original members of the Life-Saving Service at Cape Cod, Benjamin Oliver Eldridge, is still alive, so it was important to get the story of this very valuable organization before it became too late.

Together wth Richard Carlisle of Quincy, I visited Mr. Eldridge at his Cape Cod home during the summer of 1970. After interviewing him for several hours I had enough background so that, by adding information from several other sources, I can relate the story of the Life-Saving Service of this country.

In the year 1807 the Massachusetts Humane Society erected, near Cohasset, a station fitted with a lifeboat. Previous to this time there were along the coast of the United States no houses equipped with even the crudest apparatus for the saving of life. In 1787 there were only three huts of refuge which the shipwrecked sailor could reach, one on Lovell's Island, another on Nantasket Beach, and a third at Scituate. All were built in that year by the Massachusetts Humane Society.

A shipwreck in 1803, however, disclosed an unenviable situation, for the Society discovered there were moon cussers and vandals all along the coast even then. Handicapped because of its relative inexperience in shipwreck matters, a committee of the Humane Society Trustees "appointed to enquire into, and publish a state of facts respecting the preservation of a number of persons by the Society's Hut on Nantasket Beach," set forth in the following statement how much help was needed:

THAT Capt. William Gibson of the brigantine *Elizabeth*, bound from *St. Vincents* to *Boston*, consigned to Mr. David Green, arrived in the Bay on Dec. 15; that Mr. Thomas Knox, jun. the Pilot, went on board her at 11 o'clock P.M. then in the Light-House-Channel, and found her in a very disabled condition; That at 2 o'clock A.M. of the 16th, the wind coming to the North West, and blowing almost a hurricane, the brigantine parted her cable, and drifted till 2 o'clock P.M. when she struck on *Point Alderton Bar*.

The sea beating entirely over her, and the brig striking very hard, four of the hands, much fatigued, and overcome by the excessive cold, committed themselves to the mercy of the waves, and swam to Nantasket Beach, distant about fifty yards, and proceeded to the town of *Hull;* but before they reached the houses, one of them gave out, and could not walk further, and must have perished, but for the assistance afforded him by some of the inhabitants; in consequence of intelligence received from the other three; That at 4 o'clock, P.M. the brigantine still beating upon the bar, it was expected she would go to pieces, and that there was no other alternative for those on board, but to attempt to get on shore or to perish; some of them thought that in their debilitated and almost frozen condition they should never be able to reach the shore. Mr. Knox, however, made the attempt, and taking with him the end of a deep sea line, the other end of which was fastened to the bodies of the others, he swam to the beach and drew them on shore. Upon getting ashore, they proceeded to the house erected by the Humane Society for the preservation of shipwrecked seamen.

Their cloathes wet and very much frozen, and themselves much spent, it was with great difficulty they reached the house. But who can describe their extreme grief and disappointment, when, upon their arrival, they found no fireworks, candles or straw, and but a small quantity of wood!—Capt. Gibson and Mr. Knox are, however, of opinion, that though they could not experience the salutary influence of a fire, they must have perished had it not been for the shelter afforded them by the house, from the violence of the wind and the extreme cold. Some of the inhabitants of *Hull* very humanely carried some fireworks to the house, by which means a fire was kindled, their cloathes dried, and they recovered strength sufficient, by assistance, to get to *Hull* that night, all except one man, who was too weak to make the attempt. But he was made comfortable by the fire, and other refreshment afforded by the inhabitants. This simple unadorned statement of facts, furnishes an additional evidence of the great utility which the houses erected by this society have been to that worthy and valuable part of our fellow-citizens, the mariners of our country.

And it is with great regret that your committee observe, that there are found in a civilized country, persons so abandoned and devoid of every principle of humanity, as to take from those houses, erected from principles of benevolence, to alleviate the distresses of the unfortunate shipwrecked seamen, the tinderbox, candles, straw and fuel, with which they are supplied every year by this society, as was the case with this to which these persons resorted; and thereby leave these distressed people to perish for want of articles of so small value, as not to be an object worth purloining. Such inhumanity is a disgrace to any people, that are not barbarians. And the committee, in behalf of the trustees, call upon their fellow citizens of every description to detect, and they will prosecute to the utmost severity of the law, all such inhuman robbers.

JOHN LATHROP } Committee
S. PARKER

Jan. 11, 1803.

Brave men have for years, upon the approach of a storm, walked the sandy shores of Cape Cod, with no hope of pecuniary reward. The Massachusetts Humane Society, a benevolent organization, founded in the year 1785 and chartered under the laws of the state of Massachusetts in the year 1791, at first received its funds from annual subscriptions. Later on, the Society was assisted by the government and by legacies from various benefactors. By the close of 1845 the group had erected eighteen stations and huts of refuge, which the castaway might luckily see and find shelter, warmth, and dry clothing.

In 1837 Congress passed a law authorizing the sending out of revenue cutters to cruise along the coasts in stormy weather, and in the year 1848 voted ten thousand dollars for building eight stations along the New Jersey coast. In the year 1871 Congress voted "that the Secretary of the Treasury may establish such stations on the coasts of Long Island and New Jersey for aiding shipwrecked vessels thereon, and furnish such apparatus and supplies as may in his judgment be best adapted to the preservation of life and property from such shipwrecked vessels."

From this time dates the beginning of the present Life-Saving Service of the United States.

The estimated number of lives saved and the amount of property rescued during the years from November 1, 1871, to June 30, 1889, inclusive, when a special survey was made, was: Total number of persons rescued, 42,359; total number lost, 505; total value of property saved, $60,352,092.

For the year ending June 30, 1889, from a total of 3384 lives involved, 3068 were saved. The value of property saved by the Service for this same length of time was $5,054,440. Of course, the importance of property fades into the background when compared with human lives.

The station at Peaked Hill Bars, Cape Cod, situated two and one-half miles from Provincetown village, was one of the most dangerous points on the Atlantic Coast. A plan of the station follows. It will give some idea of how the apparatus was kept and how the men lived who were appointed by the government to warn the sailor as his ship approached too near the shoals, and who were to be watchful and ready in the saving of life and property along the shores.

The building faced the northeast, and was forty-five feet long and forty feet wide. The distance from the sill to the ridgepole was twenty-four feet, while that from the sill to the eaves was but seven feet. The building was shingled. On the roof was a cupola lookout, from which ships hull-down could be brought into vision with the aid of telescopes.*

At the northeast corner, in a small projection facing the ocean, was the keeper's sleeping room, in which was kept the library, together with the journal of the station—a daily record of the number of passing vessels, surfmen on duty, state of the weather, and whatever of interest might take place during the day or night. The writing of the journal was mandatory.

At right angles to the keeper's room and of the same width, extending the length of the building, was a veranda, which afforded a good lookout for passing vessels. In the

* Eugene O'Neill, famed playwright, established ownership of this building when it was abandoned by the coast guard, and wrote several of his famous plays there on the Cape Cod shore.

rear of this veranda and keeper's room, separated by a partition, were the mess and boat rooms, the latter thirty feet in length and twenty feet in width, with its wide doors opening toward the southwest.

Here was kept the lifeboat, supplied with oars, ropes, and all necessary implements, mounted on its carriage ready for use at any moment. On the walls of the room were hand life-lines, belts, patrol-lanterns, working lines, blocks, and tackles, and here and there on the floor, each in its proper place, were the life-car, raft, shovels, shot-lines, faking-boxes, guns, mortars, the beach wagon loaded with apparatus, and all the equipment connected with wreck ordnance. In the rear of these rooms, extending the length of the building, also separated by a partition, were a kitchen and spare room, in which were kept the clothing, oilskins, and heavy boots worn by the crew in case of ship-wreck or inclement weather.

The keeper of a station was on duty the entire year, but was expected to be at his station only from sunset to sun-rise during the time not included in the "active season." During the "active season" he was permitted to be absent one day in each week from sunrise to sunset, provided it was pleasant weather, and he could allow each of his crew the same privilege, being careful that only one man was away at a time. In cases of sickness or leave of absence, a substitute could be employed, paid by the one whose place he took.

The surfmen were numbered, and if the keeper was sick or away, Number One took his place. Each position in the boat drilling exercise and in the handling of the beach-wagon and apparatus was designated by a number, which corresponded to the one given the surfman at his station.

The keepers of volunteer stations were required to live in the stations or in their immediate vicinity, while those in charge of houses of refuge resided in the houses the entire year. At first the pay of keepers was two hundred dollars for the "active season." Later it was increased to a sum not to exceed eight hundred dollars per year. This sum was paid only to those in charge of the most perilous stations. The majority of keepers received only seven hundred dollars per year. The wages of the surfmen were increased from thirty dollars per month to fifty dollars per month for the time included in the "active season." The salaries of the district superintendents varied from twelve hundred to eighteen hundred dollars each per year, and that of the general superintendent was four thousand.

The keepers and crew had to pay their living expenses while on duty, the government furnishing only fuel, lights, and cooking utensils. For the work performed and the perils and hardships through which they passed, they were poorly paid. However, well-endorsed petitions from all the districts, approved by the general superintendent, were forwarded in 1890 asking that Congress pass a law authorizing an increase in pay for the surfmen.

In case the keeper or one of the crew was injured while attending to his duties, and was thereby unable to perform his work, he received from the government his regular salary for a period of not more than two years. If death resulted from these injuries and he left a widow or children under sixteen years of age, they received in equal portions, for this same length of time, the salary he received while alive. If the widow married within this time, or the children attained the age of sixteen, their parts were paid to the remaining children.

Volunteer crews were subject to the rules and regulations of the service, but received no regular salary, other than a sum not to exceed eight dollars each on every occasion of actual help in case of shipwreck, and in the saving and protecting of property, a sum not to exceed three dollars per day each, at the discretion of the Secretary of the Treasury.

The surfmen patrolled the beach from two to four miles on each side of their houses four times between sunset and sunrise. In foggy weather the patrol was continued throughout the day. To patrol the beach was often a very difficult task, and attended with more or less danger. The patrolman was expected to walk the whole distance of his route, no matter how deep and blinding the snow, or how cutting the shifting sands, for along the beach gigantic masses of sand are moved with every gale. If the tide was out, the surfman walked near to the water's edge, as he had better footing, and, because of the partial shelter, escaped the full force of the wind. Of course this was dangerous, as he might suddenly be surrounded by the water, drawn back by the undertow, and eventually left on the beach a lifeless corpse. The current might carry him out to sea, where he would be buried in its fathomless depths. It was safer to walk along the high bank, which was always necessary when the tide was in, but then he had to deal with the unobstructed fury of the gale. Quite often, hiking against a terrible wind, with the sleet and sand coming at him horizontally to sting his eyes and face, he was forced to turn and walk backward as best he could.

The landmarks, whenever they could be made out in a storm, were the most commonplace—a barrel or bucket on a pole sunk into the sand at a certain spot, a keel or stern of some half-buried vessel, a mound or hollow—these told the nocturnal traveler where he was. Nevertheless, during certain great storms, the hiker on the lonely beach could be bewildered, and, after walking around, not knowing how long or where, he would be fortunate enough to get back into his station, or to be discovered and rescued from his perilous position by those sent out to bring him in from danger.

In pleasant weather a day watch was kept from the station between the morning and evening patrols, each man taking his regular turn on all watches and patrols.

On patrols two men would start out in opposite directions from each station; one would walk the beach to the left, while the other proceeded to the right. Each would continue on his lonely way until the end of the beat was reached. The boundary mark was generally a post or small hut, a shelter from the cutting winds. In some cases, at the meeting-places there were small cabins, half-buried in the sand; inside were stoves in which the patrolman who arrived first would build a fire, which was kept burning through the night. Here the patrolmen from adjacent stations met each other, each man often bringing a small quantity of fuel. After a short chat and an exchange of metal discs, or checks, given them by their respective keepers on leaving for patrol, they returned to their stations, their watches having expired, bringing the checks received, showing that they had gone over their whole distance, and that all was well along the shore.

The check was a small square piece of brass, pierced with a hole; and on it was stamped the name of the station and the number corresponding to the surfman's number at his station. The checks collected during the night were returned by the first watch the following night to the stations from which they were sent.

At isolated stations a patrol clock was used, which registered the time when the end of the route was reached. The solitary traveler would start out, taking with him the clock fastened to his person by a strap. At the end of his patrol was a small iron box placed either in a hole dug for the purpose or on a post. Inside the box was a key that wound the clock. With a key brought from the station he would open this box and by means of the one found inside wind the clock. A small hole was made in the dial, showing the time he arrived. After replacing the key and locking the box, he would return. At twelve o'clock at night the keeper would take out the old dial and in its place put a new one. The old dials were sent with the daily report of the station to the district superintendent.

If after waiting at a halfway house a suitable length of time the watch from the adjacent station failed to appear, the one already there would proceed toward the station to meet him, lest, bewildered, he had lost his way and perished on the beach, or perhaps had discovered a shipwrecked vessel.

A patrolman often carried with him a beach-lantern, but always Coston signals, which he would instantly light upon noticing a vessel too near the shore, to warn those on board of their danger, and in case of shipwrecks to give them courage by assuring them that they were seen and that assistance was not far away. This light would burn for two minutes, sending up a bright red flame that could be seen at a long distance. If a keeper of one station wished to notify the neighboring station of a wreck and ask for aid, he would burn a red rocket. The patrolman seeing this would answer with a white rocket. After showing his red light to a stranded vessel, the patrolman with all speed would hurry back to the house and arouse its inmates.

Immediately upon the cry of "Ship ashore!" each man was ready for duty. The crews were regularly drilled in the use of the beach-apparatus, as well as in the handling of the lifeboat, so that there was no misunderstanding of what should be done or who should do it. Each man had his particular work to do and did it readily, thereby saving time when it was most needed.

The crews were also instructed in the restoring of the apparently drowned and in the treatment of frostbites. Some stations had besides the lifeboat a surfboat. If it was expedient to use the large lifeboat, it was soon at the water's edge, ready to be pushed off and rowed by strong arms to the scene of disaster. If the surfboat could be of service, it was drawn as quickly as possible over the beach toward the ill-fated vessel, and launched from the most available point. The surfboat was built more like an ordinary rowboat, and was used principally in drilling exercises and in boarding vessels during moderate weather.

At times, when the boats could not be used, the wreck-gun and beach-apparatus, together with the breeches-buoy or the life-car, were brought into service. The breeches-buoy, being much lighter and more easily handled than the life-car, was more often used. It was made of heavy duck, and resembled a pair of knee pants, having two openings through which the legs were extended, and around the upper part, or waistband, was fastened a large piece of cork, which served as a buoy. When the breeches-buoy was used, the survivor thrust both legs through the openings made for that purpose, and clung to the ropes attached to the buoy and leading from a traveler block suspended from a hawser.

The gun most commonly used in getting a hawser to a ship was the "Lyle," a small brass cannon 22 inches long and with 2½-inch bore, which would shoot a shot weighing 18 pounds. Tied to this shot was a small shot-line, which was attached to the hawser.

Soon after being patented in June 1887, the "Hunt" gun and projectiles were introduced. In the projectile was coiled a small line, to which was tied the short shot-line. The guns were of about the same size and were similarly loaded and fired, the one shooting a shot, and the other the projectile. A friction primer was placed in the vent, and the drawing taut of a line fastened to the primer caused the explosion. The guns could be raised or lowered to any desired angle. The particular advantage claimed by the Hunt projectiles over the old-style guns was that the shot-line, a small line of linen, was simply uncoiled and left behind in its flight, while the other guns, in shooting, had to drag the line through the air. In case the shot-line on the projectile should not work favorably, a second line, on a reel, was placed near the gun. The ends of this second line and the shot-line were tied together before the gun was fired.

Small mounds of earth and marble slabs now mark the places where many Life-Savers are buried. What more suitable epitaph could be carved than the words telling that they died in saving others, what more eloquent eulogy pronounced than that in time of great danger they were not found wanting in the performance of their duty?

XIV

Cape Cod Wrecks

A THREE-BARGE DISASTER

Barges were an important part of shipping in the period between 1890 and 1920. Schooners had outlived their usefulness, and scores of them every year were converted into barges to be towed up and down the Atlantic Coast. Usually each barge had a captain, and often there were several in the crew. The tugs that pulled them made up the tow with two, three, and sometimes four barges.

My book *A Pilgrim Returns to Cape Cod* shows a picture of three barges that were wrecked on Cape Cod. I was never able to tell the story in the fullness it deserves, but now, with the aid of the last living Life-Saver of Cape Cod, Benjamin Oliver Eldridge, I can give in detail what occurred when the wreck took place.

On the evening of January 6, 1911, the tug *Lykens* * set out from Philadelphia with three coal-laden barges in tow,

---

* Built at Philadelphia in 1899, she had a gross tonnage of 625, was 157 feet long, had a beam of 29 feet, and a depth of hold of 17.5 feet.

the *Pine Forest,* the *Corbin,* and the *Trevorton.* Their cargoes were consigned to parties in Salem, Portsmouth, and Portland.

The tug and tow made good weather of it until they arrived off Highland Light on the coast of Massachusetts' Cape Cod on the evening of January 9, when they ran into a strong west-northwest wind. Fearing for the safety of his tow, the master of the tug, Captain Francis E. Hammond, altered his course soon after encountering the gale, turning farther to the westward, with the intention of pulling across Cape Cod to Plymouth, from which place the voyage, he concluded, could be continued with less risk under the shelter of the land.

After passing Highland Light, Captain Hammond noticed that the wind hauled more to the northward and freshened up considerably, and the sea became very rough, both of which, combined with the tide setting out strong from the bay, made the progress of the vessels almost impossible.

By midnight the wind had attained a velocity of about sixty miles an hour, and the vessels were practically hove to. When the tide turned at one o'clock, Captain Hammond decided to risk everything because of the gravity of the situation and attempt to get his tow into the bay. He started ahead again under all the steam the *Lykens* could raise.

So terrible did the gale become that after an hour they had covered barely a mile. While the barges were laboring heavily, as was disclosed by the searchlight from the tug, they were holding their own, and there seemed to be a fair chance that they would all get around Race Point and reach the relative shelter of Massachusetts Bay.

Shortly after quarter past four that morning the aft watch on the *Lykens* called the master with a report that the number one tow, immediately behind them, was signaling with a light. The captain came out on deck to see what the matter was. Following the ray of the searchlight with his glasses, he took a careful look at the vessel, but only her side lights were visible.

The captain had hardly gone inside again when the tug gave a lurch forward. The strain on her towing hawser had suddenly eased. Almost at once she slowed into her regular speed. Then, a few moments later, she shot forward again in the same manner. Several of the *Lykens'* crew ran aft at once to find out what the trouble was and discovered that the hawser board had worked free and fallen inside the taffrail. While engaged in replacing the board, they noticed that the tug was again going ahead at greatly increased speed. This meant but one thing—the *Lykens* had lost all three barges in the gale.

Slowing down the *Lykens,* Captain Hammond ordered all hands on deck to pull in the hawser. As the last fragment of cable came aboard, it was found that the entire line and even the towing bridle attached to the outer end were intact, indicating that the bridle had worked loose from its fastenings aboard the barge, slipped through the chocks and dropped into the sea—doubtless without the knowledge of anybody on board.

As soon as the hawser was pulled in and made secure on board, the captain ordered the *Lykens* swung around to go back in search of the lost tow. After cruising up and down the coast from Peaked Hill Bars to Race Point, she came across the *Pine Forest,* the sternmost barge in line. It was daybreak, and those on the *Lykens* sighted the *Pine Forest* lying in the surf. The tug could find no trace of the two other vessels, however, which led the master to hope against hope that they had succeeded in weathering the cape.

The gale was still driving with terrible force, and the

water on all sides of the stranded vessel was a veritable caldron of boiling seas. In the opinion of Captain Hammond nothing could be done to help the barge, for to have ventured into the broken water surrounding her would have jeopardized the lives of all twenty men in his own crew.

While this drama was being enacted offshore, the life-saving crews from Peaked Hill Bars and Race Point were trudging along the beach with their apparatus. They noticed that the tug was leaving the wrecked barge and watched her as she left the area making no signals at all. The *Lykens* ran into Provincetown Harbor, where some hours later the captain learned the fate of the other vessels.

What actually befell the *Trevorton* and *Corbin* after the towline parted can only be surmised, as no one in any of the three barges lived to tell his story. It is believed that the *Trevorton* and the *Corbin* drifted together and hammered each other to pieces.

The *Pine Forest,* the last barge in the line, probably snapped her hawser and drifted away from the others, or else she was much the stauncher craft of the three. In any event, wind and buffeting seas swept her shoreward intact and set her hard and fast in that graveyard of ships, the outlying sands of Cape Cod. There, several hundred yards from the beach, she was noticed at break of day with the seas sweeping over her amidships.

Had the sailors remained by her, as instructed to do by the life-saving crews standing by on the beach, every man of them eventually would have been saved. The responsibility for what followed their disregard of the warning given them is placed where it belongs by the owners of the barges in a report that contains the following:

The attempt of the captain and crew to launch a small dory in spite of the warnings of the life-saving crews on shore was suicidal. The entire five men on board were drowned as a result of their own actions. Had they stuck to their vessel all would have been saved during the day of January 10, as the life-saving crews could easily have taken them off when the gale subsided. The cause of the accident to the barges will never be known. The disconnection of the hawser occurred on the foremost barge, but how, no man can say. The secret was buried with the lost men.

Ashore on the beach Surfman Higgins, of the Peaked Hill Bars Life-Saving Station, first saw the barges two hours or more before disaster overtook them. At the time Higgins was making his patrol eastward and noticed that the craft were going along slowly, showing only the usual lights and with no sign of trouble.

They were next observed by Surfman Carlos, of the same station, who set out on the west patrol at quarter to four. When five hundred yards or more from the station, Carlos discovered the lights of three or four craft near the bars. After satisfying himself that the vessels were in dangerous waters, he burned two Coston lights to warn them of their peril. He then ran back to his station and gave the alarm.

Surfman William E. Silvey was temporarily in charge of the life-saving crew, as Keeper William W. Cook was home in Provincetown on twenty-four-hour liberty. Silvey accompanied Carlos a short way up the beach to confirm his report, and sighted a vessel apparently at anchor outside the bar, while farther westward and nearer the beach, in the locality of the Halfway House, the lights of two other craft could be seen.

The surfmen returned to the station and turned out the others in the crew. Then they telephoned the news to the keeper of the Race Point Station, three miles westward. All hands now set out with the beach apparatus. After an hour's torturing work pulling the apparatus along the beach, they arrived abeam of the craft whose lights Higgins had first detected. The Race Point crew arrived on the scene ten minutes later.

By this time the vessel first seen, and which proved to be the *Pine Forest,* was lying more than a quarter of a mile from the beach, apparently fast on the offshore bar. Some distance outside was another vessel throwing a searchlight on the *Forest.* The lights of the craft sighted farther along the beach were no longer visible.

Silvey and his men continued walking westward in an effort to find some trace of the vessels that had disappeared and were joined near the Halfway House by the men from Race Point Station coming east. When the two crews met, Captain Samuel O. Fisher, of the Race Point Station, took command. The entire group set out to the eastward where lay the one vessel whose lights were still in view.

They had gone only a short distance through the breaking dawn when a vessel's hull was seen offshore. Telling Silvey to keep on until he should come abreast of the vessel, Captain Fisher unloaded the apparatus with the intention of shooting a line over the object. He placed the gun in position, loaded it with six ounces of powder, attached a No. 9 line to the projectile, and was on the point of pulling the lanyard when a surfman shouted: "She's gone!"

Nevertheless, Captain Fisher fired into the dawn. The crew waited awhile but received no responsive pull. The line was then hauled in. As there was nothing any longer visible to hit, the men reloaded the apparatus on the wagon and the tramp eastward was resumed.

When Silvey arrived abreast of the one remaining vessel, the *Pine Forest,* she was still where she had been when he passed her the first time. Although she lay at a great distance from the shore, out of range of the wreck gun, and the wind was blowing directly across the line of fire, a shot was taken. The line failed to carry to the vessel. Three more shots were fired, every one ending in failure.

Becoming convinced of the futility of further effort with gun and line, Captain Fisher now decided to try to reach the barge by boat. Two men were accordingly dispatched to the Race Point Station for the surfboat. Another group started for the Peaked Hill Station. The boat from the last-named station arrived first and was made ready for launching. A half hour later the other boat also arrived, and was likewise run down to the water.

Still at its height, the storm was sending towering waves rolling in, twenty feet high. In spite of wind and sea, however, the men on the beach gathered around the boat from Peaked Hill Bars and ran it into the water. They had scarcely succeeded in shoving its nose into the first breaking sea when they were hurled off their feet and flung helter-skelter back on the beach. Several times they attempted to launch, each time with the same result.

Out on the barge in the gathering daylight the men were seen to make for a boat suspended from davits, get into it, and start to lower it. Before they could free it of its lashings, however, a sea broke over the barge, swept across the deck, and poured a solid wall of water over the rail and into the boat, filling it and half-drowning the occupants. After the sea passed they all clambered out and hoisted the boat by its bow, evidently to drain it. Then they went and stood in the shelter of the house as if to debate what to do next.

When it was seen what the sailors were planning, one of the men on the beach ran and got the necessary flags from the apparatus cart and waved the signal: "Do not attempt to land; unsafe." Apparently to signify that the warning had been understood, one of the sailors stepped toward the rail and waved his hand.

The surfmen turned to launching their boat, but suddenly they noticed the bargemen were again active. The sailors had witnessed the efforts of the life-saving crews to get away from the shore. Probably afraid that their barge would soon break up to drop them to their death in the surf, they now turned to the dory again. This time they got it over the side and free of its lashings, but forgot to unship their oars, stowed under the thwarts, so that when the boat struck the water they could not propel it. As it was, they hardly seated themselves before the boat was swept out past the vessel's stern, where a sea caught it up and capsized it.

Every sailor wore a cork life jacket. Three of them regained the boat and managed to hold to it for a brief interval as it drifted eastward in the swift longshore current. The others, helped by their jackets, kept their heads up, but the chill of the water and smother of the breakers exhausted them one by one, and they collapsed and perished.

Captain Fisher now sent several surfmen along the beach with grapnels and heaving sticks, in readiness to rescue any of the sailors who might float within reach. The boat, free of those who had managed to swim back to it after it upset, came ashore first. Its oars were still tucked under the thwarts.

Keeper Cook, of the Peaked Hill Bars Station, who reached the scene of the disaster about 9 A.M. in response to a telephone message, saw one of the sailors about twenty yards off making a valiant effort to reach land. Everyone on the beach shouted to him to keep swimming and they would soon get him, but before he came near enough for them to get hold of him, his head dropped forward and he ceased to struggle. When hauled out shortly afterward, he was dead. The surfmen worked for nearly an hour in an unsuccessful effort to revive him. He was the first man to be taken from the water.

The bodies of the others came ashore one by one to the eastward in the next hour. Altogether, the bodies of fifteen of the seventeen men who perished from the three barges were finally recovered. The 1763-ton *Trevorton* carried seven men, the 954-ton *Corbin* and the 901-ton *Pine Forest* had as their crew five men each. All three vessels were owned by the Philadelphia & Reading Coal Company.

Those who perished were Captain Frederick I. Brown of the *Trevorton* and his crew, Dominico Milosecic, Andrew Olsen, Victor Sanstrom, Albert Sorensen, Fred Hausen, and William Walham. From the *Corbin* there were Captain Charles N. Smith, Charles E. Smith, John Hendrickson, Alfred Olsen, and Anton Pedersen. Those aboard the *Pine Forest* were Captain Monroe W. Hall, William Wicks, John Gardos, Clarence B. Burns, and Einar Hjorth.

The pages of the Boston *Herald* for January 12, 1911, include the report of Captain Hammond of the *Lykens*. Later the captain was exonerated, and it was agreed that he was in no way responsible for what was declared an act of God.

Captain Hammond stated: "I slowed the tug down and ordered the watch below on deck to get our hawser in, putting the wheel to port so as to keep an eye on the barges from the pilothouse. A little later I was obliged to go stronger on the engine to give us steerage way, and so lost sight of the tow before I got the hawser in."

THE BARGES *GIRARD* AND *ALASKA*

At six-thirty in the morning on February 18, 1907, while making his north patrol, Surfman Antone T. Lucas of

Cape Cod's Highland Life-Saving Station discovered a wreck about a mile or so north of the station.

It was the barge *Girard*. Broadside to the sea, the *Girard* was "making very bad weather of it."

It all began on February 14, 1907, when the tug *Valley Forge* left Philadelphia with a string of barges, the *Bethayres, Alaska,* and *Girard,* laden with coal consigned to the Consumers Coal Company of Boston.

The 824-ton *Girard* was a three-masted, schooner-rigged vessel carrying 900 tons of coal and drawing twelve feet. Her sails and rigging were in good condition, and her hatches well secured, covered with tarpaulins and battened down with wedges and bars. She was in good condition and well prepared for heavy weather.

The *Valley Forge* and her tow were attended by good weather until they arrived off Cape Cod on the morning of the eighteenth, passing the Pollock Rip lightship about 3 A.M. Here the four vessels ran into a northeast gale, which rapidly increased from thirty-five to no less than sixty-five miles an hour. The wind blew directly on shore and was accompanied by thick snow squalls and extremely cold weather.

When the tug had forced its way with the barges to a point about six miles north of the Highland Life-Saving Station, the line connecting the *Bethayres* with the *Alaska* snapped, setting the latter vessel and the *Girard* adrift.

Separated from their tow, the two barges, still with a line between them, drifted to leeward, their bows to the northwest. Half an hour later it was agreed that the hawser should be cast off from the *Alaska*, permitting each vessel to follow her own course.

As soon as the master of the *Girard*—a young Norwegian named Larsen—saw that he was adrift from the *Alaska*, he set up his forestaysail and foresail, hauling the sheets aft to the port side to force her head around to the wind. The vessel would not mind her sail, however, but fell off to leeward instead, and headed toward shore.

Suddenly the snow thinned, disclosing breakers ahead. To avoid getting into the breakers, Captain Larsen ordered sail taken in. Both the starboard and the port anchors were let go with sixty fathoms of chain on each. At first the ground tackle did not hold, and she continued to drag toward the breakers on the outer bar, not quite a mile offshore. The *Girard* finally worked over the bar, after pounding on it so hard that her timbers cracked.

A sea now came aboard and picked up seaman Gustaf Johannesen, who was standing amidships, and carried him away. Cook Martin Berg saw him go and threw overboard a ring life buoy and a life preserver, but both fell short. The two other men on board—Captain Larsen and seaman Joe Johnson—were too busy looking out for their own safety and trying to manage the barge to do anything for their unfortunate shipmate. Being heavily clad, Johannesen was never seen again.

When the *Girard* hit the bar and hove across, she brought up on her cables and held for half an hour. The seas beat heavily against her and washed over her. Before long the breakers stove in her hatches, and water began to fill her hold. This brought her so low in the water that she began to pound again and started to drag toward the inner bar. Soon she went over the inner bar and reached the breakers, two hundred yards from the beach, bringing up broadside to the sea with her bow to the south.

Berg and Johnson were in the pilothouse when the barge made her last stand. Both of them by this time were suffering severely from cold. The master, who had remained on deck up to this moment, now climbed on top of the pilothouse, where he might the better take in their desperate situation and consider what could be done under the circumstances.

Back on shore, Surfman Lucas first sighted the *Girard* at this moment. He abandoned his patrol and ran to the nearby Halfway House, from which place he telephoned to his keeper. Lucas then retraced his steps to the station. Within a few minutes after his arrival, his comrades harnessed the station horse and began to fight their way along the beach, using all their strength to help the horse pull the apparatus cart. They arrived abeam of the *Girard* just as she came ashore, and were soon joined by the High Head Station crew, to whom Acting Keeper McFayden of the Highland Station had sent notice.

Ten minutes after the Highland Life-Savers reached the scene, a Number 9 shot-line was sent across the two hundred yards of surf intervening between the shore and the barge. It fell so close to the captain on top of the pilothouse that all he had to do was reach out and lay hold of it.

Having caught the line, Captain Larsen called Berg and Johnson from their shelter to help him haul the tackle on board. This work accomplished, the whip-line block was made fast around the framework of the house between the two forward windows, the window sash being kicked out for the purpose. Upon a signal from Larsen, the men on the beach then hauled off the hawser, which was made fast on the barge by hitching it around the pilothouse.

The apparatus having been set up on the shore, the breeches-buoy was now hauled off. Larsen ordered the cook to get into it, but the man was so benumbed by cold that he could no longer do anything to help himself. The master of the *Girard* was forced to pick him up bodily and put him in the breeches-buoy.

When Cook Berg started shoreward, Johnson went back into the pilothouse and stripped off his outer clothing, probably to enable him the better to cope with the seas when his turn should come to get into the buoy. But the weather was bitterly cold, and he had already been drenched to the skin while out on deck. When the breeches-buoy came out the second time, Johnson was found by the captain, unconscious and hanging to the wheel with his arms around the spokes in such a way that he could not be pulled loose.

Larsen himself was rapidly freezing. He realized that if he waited on the barge he also soon would be unconscious. Therefore, he reluctantly left the insensible man to his fate. Stumbling out of the pilothouse, he made his way along the unstable deck to the waiting breeches-buoy. Then, with great difficulty, he managed to get in and signal for his rescuers to haul away. He was soon in the hands of the Life-Savers, but just in time. Scarcely had the breeches-buoy passed over the water when the *Girard* began to break up, and within fifteen to twenty minutes she was scattered and strewn in small fragments along the beach.

The Highland crew hastened back to their station with the *Girard*'s cook lying in the apparatus cart. He had been taken from the breeches-buoy unconscious. Larsen followed on foot, assisted by a surfman. After the clothing of the survivors had been removed, they were given stimulants. The prescribed treatment for frostbite was then administered, and they were put to bed. A physician from Provincetown then took charge.

The High Head Life-Savers had, on their way back from the *Girard*, sighted the *Alaska* through the snow flurries. She was then at anchor outside the outer bar. Now they returned to the beach to look for her. On reaching their station they could see from the shore that the *Alaska* was shipping a great deal of water, but was apparently holding on in spite of the weather. They reported their discovery by telephone to the Highland crew, who pulled their cart one and a quarter miles north from the Highland Station and abreast of the *Alaska,* in readiness if she should strike or come close enough to permit shooting a line across her.

At about 1:00 P.M. the *Alaska* was observed dragging to leeward. Suddenly she foundered and settled in four fathoms just outside the outer bar, three fourths of a mile offshore. No signs of life were at any time visible from the beach.

The theory is that the seas stove in the hatches of the *Alaska* and filled her hold. No rescuing boat, had there been one at hand, could have reached her under the prevailing conditions. The distance she lay offshore also prevented the use of the beach apparatus. There was, therefore, no way in which the Life-Saving crews on the beach could have helped the men on the *Alaska.*

As was the case with the *Girard,* the terrible pounding broke her up a very short time after she settled. For two or three hours the Life-Savers kept a close watch on the beach for possible survivors or dead bodies. None came ashore, however, and the Life-Savers returned to their stations, chilled, hungry, and exhausted from their nine hours' work in the winter storm.

It was afterward ascertained that the crew of the *Alaska* consisted of four persons—the master, cook, and two deck hands—not one of whom was ever seen again.

The tug *Valley Forge* and the barge *Bethayres* were found fifty miles offshore, where they had successfully ridden out the storm.

THE BARGE *COLERAINE*

The barge *Coleraine* was one of three which left Bangor, Maine, in April 1915, bound for Philadelphia. Towed out of Bangor Harbor by the tug *Mars*, the barges encountered heavy weather as the four vessels approached Cape Cod. The following day it began to snow, with the wind setting in from the northeast. At six o'clock that afternoon the captain noticed white water ahead, and realized that he was nearing the Cape. He ordered the cables to the barges cut, changed the tug's course, and a few hours later anchored in Provincetown Harbor, where his propeller dropped off.

The three barges, the *Coleraine*, the *Tunnel Ridge*, and the *Manheim*, now began to drift against the shores of Cape Cod. One by one they grounded in the sands, but the *Tunnel Ridge* and the *Coleraine* were badly damaged before they hit the beach. The other vessel, in command of Captain George Israel, let go both her anchors, delaying the action of the sea in pushing her up on the beach. By the time she joined the other barges on the shore, the storm had begun to abate, so that the *Manheim* was still in good condition.

The action of the sea soon built up a great breakwater of sand around the *Tunnel Ridge* and the *Coleraine*, which were lying stranded one on each side of the *Manheim*. Thus it was impossible to try to float off the uninjured *Manheim* until the two badly wrecked barges were disposed of. It was finally decided to set fire to the wrecked vessels after Captain Israel had allowed the men of Cape Cod to take off the deckhouses from the *Coleraine*. The houses were landed on the beach, cut into smaller sections, and pulled up the steep sides of the Highland cliff by four horses. Made into a three-room building, one soon bore the name of the "Highland House Golf Links."

On the fourth day of April 1916 the barge *Manheim* was towed off the beach at Cape Cod. Just a year had elapsed since the wreck of the vessel.

THE ITALIAN BARK *GIOVANNI*

In the winter of 1875 the Italian bark *Giovanni* sailed from Palermo with a cargo of sumac, nuts, and brimstone. On March 4, running into a northeast storm off Cape Cod, she drove upon the outer sand bar three miles north of the Highland Life-Saving Station. The crew from the station, unable to launch their boat into the mountainous breakers, set up their mortar gun on the beach.

Few thought that the gun could carry to the vessel in the face of that terrific gale, but several attempts were made before the project was abandoned. The bark was seen to be breaking up. Two men jumped from the wheelhouse to the wreckage that was beginning to float ashore. One of them soon disappeared from view. The other slowly drifted ashore, where the Life-Savers rushed into the sea, joining hands until they formed a living rope. Soon the breakers forced him near the beach, and the foremost man in the chain pulled him from the raging surf.

All that night long huge bonfires burned on the beach to give hope and encouragement to the survivors on the wreck. The next day a man was seen to jump from the bow of the vessel and swim to the deckhouse, there to join three of his companions. Soon afterward the *Giovanni* went to pieces. Although two of the men clung to wreckage until they were halfway ashore, their strength then failed and they sank beneath the waves. The drama of the *Giovanni* was over.

Only that first Italian sailor was rescued from the fifteen on board the *Giovanni*. No other person, dead or alive, ever came ashore from the bark.

THE *MONTE TABOR*

The loss of the Italians aboard the bark *Monte Tabor,*
wrecked on the Peaked Hill Bars of Cape Cod on September 14, 1896, became an unsolved mystery of the sea. Although the loss of life was comparatively small, the shipwreck remained a puzzle to the men of the Cape.

The *Monte Tabor,* hailing from Genoa, was loaded with
salt from Trapani, Sicily. Struck by a hurricane on September 9, she was trying to make Provincetown Harbor at the
time she hit the bars.

Patrolman Silvey of the Peaked Hill Life-Saving Station
discovered the wreck, but it was impossible to launch the
lifeboat. The bark's cabin broke away from the vessel and
carried six of the crew ashore to safety. Another young
Italian, who reached land by swimming, hid in the beach
plum bushes until taken by the Life-Savers. He explained
that he expected to be killed if shipwrecked at Cape Cod,
which was what the others aboard had told him.

Of those who did not reach land, three committed suicide, according to survivors from the bark, while the remainder of the crew disappeared in the storm. Some say
that the captain was so humiliated at the loss of his fine
vessel that he killed himself, and two of the other officers
followed his example. At the time the survivors claimed
it was an Italian custom for the captain of a wrecked craft
to take his own life.

THE *CAPE ANN*

At three o'clock in the morning, March 6, 1948, during
a bad easterly gale which brought high winds and roaring

surf, the 82-foot scallop dragger *Cape Ann* pounded in over the shoals off Nauset Beach Light, Cape Cod, and stranded in the midst of the great breakers surging against the cliff below the lighthouse.

The *Cape Ann* had been bound for New Bedford with a capacity cargo of scallops.

First to detect the lights of the vessel in the darkness of that March night was Coast Guardsman Harold Stafford, on duty at the Nauset Beach tower about three miles away.

As soon as it became known that a dragger was ashore, help began to converge on the area from all directions. At that time the rescue craft *General Greene* was proceeding to the assistance of another fishing boat, the *Gay Head,* crippled off Nantucket. The *Greene* immediately changed her course to go to the aid of the *Cape Ann.*

When the *Greene* arrived just seaward of the wrecked craft, the sailors put over a lifeboat and rowed as close as they could to her, but the great breaking waves kept them at least 150 yards away.

Meanwhile, crews from all available Coast Guard stations were arriving on the scene. Within a relatively short time they set up a Lyle gun on top of the eighty-foot cliff.

Most of the crew of the dragger had been asleep when the helmsman of the heavily loaded fishing craft had apparently taken Nauset Beach Light for the Pollock Rip Lightship. Jumping from their beds, they were soon in the rigging, which was heavily coated with ice in the below-freezing weather. From there they watched the Coast Guard efforts high on the cliff ashore.

When the first shot from the Lyle gun was sent out, the men were dismayed to see it land out of reach in the sea a few yards away from them.

The second shot was successful, for after making a 400-foot parabola above them, the line dropped across the rigging of the wave-swept dragger. Soon it was made firm to the foretop crosstree and the breeches-buoy was sent out. One after another the crew left the craft. Finally all of the crew had reached safety except for the captain, the engineer, the cook, and the mate.

Then the seas subsided with surprising rapidity. The danger appeared to have passed, but, as all men of the sea realize, there was nothing to prevent the storm from returning with renewed vigor. If it did, the *Cape Ann,* which had already bilged, might go to pieces, losing the four men still aboard.

The Coast Guard could not officially demand that the captain leave his own vessel, regardless of the seriousness of the occasion, and he and the three others refused to take advantage of the rescuers' efforts.

Fortunately the tide went down and the *Cape Ann* was left stranded on the beach.

Aside from salvaging the cargo, equipment, and machinery, there wasn't much that could be done about the *Cape Ann* and she was finally abandoned on the shore.

XV

⚓

A Horrible Ending

Shipwrecks of unusual nature have always fascinated me, but without question the results of the stranding of the barque *Granicus* in 1829 led to as weird and horrible a result as any of the hundreds of marine disasters about which I have written.

On charts and maps Anticosti Island resembles a huge seal swimming through the gulf toward the St. Lawrence River. Situated directly in the mouth of the river, the island lies entirely between the forty-ninth and fiftieth degrees of latitude and is 136 miles long and thirty-five miles wide.

A large part of the island coast has a belt of limestone reefs which are bare at low water, making it difficult for the mariner to reach a safe harbor in time of storm. The only suitable harbor is at Gamache Bay, also called Ellis Bay, and it is there that Port Menier is located.

The southern part of the island is fairly low-lying, but on the north, cliffs rise to heights of four hundred and five hundred feet. The highest point is believed to be at Cape

Observation, 625 feet above the waters of the gulf. The coastal rocks in the vicinity and in many other parts of the island are covered with a dense forest of dwarf spruce trees with gnarled and twisted branches so thick a man can walk along on top of them. Birch, spruce, and, surprisingly enough, southern pine grow in the interior of the island.

Anticosti was discovered by Cartier in 1534, and named by him Assumption Island. In 1542 pilot Jean Alphonse called it Ascension Isle. But the Indians who lived peacefully along the shores of the island in those days always referred to it as Natiscotee, and Spanish fishermen corrupted the Indian name to Anticosti.

Louis XIV granted the fief or feudal estate of the island to Sieur Louis Joliet in 1680 as a reward for his discovery of the Mississippi River. Joliet was captured in 1690 by the Phips expedition out of Boston, which made a vain attempt to storm Quebec, but Phips finally released Joliet, and allowed him to return to his island fastness. Later that same year, a member of the Phips expedition, Captain John Rainsford of Boston, was wrecked at Anticosti, and we shall hear more of his story further on in this chapter.

Eventually, members of the Forsyth family acquired possession of Anticosti. In 1825 it was annexed to Lower Canada by an act of Parliament, and in 1895 Henri Meunier, the chocolate king of France, purchased the island for the sum of $125,000.

When I set out to pursue the story of the *Granicus,* Anticosti presented many transportation problems to me. Finally I was able to arrange for the trip in successive stages by plane, car, and boat.

Landing at the airport in Moncton, New Brunswick, I went overland by car until I reached the Gaspé Peninsula. It was a rough and bumpy ride over roads that time and again showed their best days had passed. But at last I ar-

rived at a little fishing village and asked one of the natives
to take me to the home of a fisherman who had a boat I
could charter. Soon I was introduced to Pierre Gaudette
and inspected his fishing craft. It seemed quite suitable for
my projected journey and I decided to make arrangements
with its owner.

When Pierre Gaudette learned that I merely planned to
sail out around Cape Gaspé, cross over to Anticosti and
cruise along the shore beyond East Cape to Fox Bay, he
could hardly believe his ears. He was certain that I must
have some ulterior motive for the trip—perhaps smuggling
dope or contraband arms. But he agreed to make the voyage as I outlined it on my chart.

Seven hours later, as we approached Heath Point Light,
we ran into a thick fog. Just beyond the lighthouse is
Wreck Bay, the scene of the amazing story of the barque
Granicus, and it was there I wished to land. An hour later
we could see the shore at Merrimack Point, and the fog
cleared enough for us to distinguish the beacon at Reef
Point, marking the southern entrance to Fox Bay. In the
distance was a tiny river, with another beacon on a small
headland that jutted out into the bay to the northeast of
the stream. Luckily, the tide was coming in, and my escort
decided to maneuver up the bay as far as he dared.

Now the engine began to skip, and Pierre finally stopped
the craft altogether and let it drift slowly toward the beach.

"You take small boat and go ashore?" Gaudette suggested.

I thrilled at the chance. Anticosti laws are very strict,
and anyone who goes ashore without permission will be
in trouble, but if a shipwrecked mariner finds himself off
the shore, he is able to use the island in the emergency.
So, being stranded, I was perfectly entitled to go ashore
and look for help.

My real reason for landing on the island was that I wished to see the little enclosure where the victims from the barque *Granicus* had been buried. Then I wished to try to find the old house or refuge nearby where the terrible deed had been perpetrated.

Landing on the beach, I pulled the dory high above the reach of the water and had soon climbed up to Fox Point headland, a cliff about fifty feet high. When I found a small enclosed cemetery plot, I realized that I had accomplished half of my objective; here were the *Granicus* graves.

But I still wanted to visit the old house of refuge. On and on I trudged, but there were no buildings in sight. Then, as I came out into a clearing, in the distance I could see Table Head Lighthouse, just to the right of a headland 260 feet high. I began to walk in its direction.

Before I could reach the lighthouse, however, a foghorn blast sounded behind me. It was Pierre's signal that we must be starting back to the Gaspé. I knew that I had already gone too far from Fox Bay and that the fog might come in again so I hurried back to the beach and the dory. It was not long before Pierre Gaudette and I started for Gaspé.

Pierre, still suspicious of my motives, was ready with his queries. "What you do on island? Tell me truth!" he began. "Why you take so long to come back?"

Pierre understood English fairly well, and I decided to tell him the entire fiendish story of the *Granicus*, my chief reason for visiting Anticosti.

While I talked, the fog drifted in and across us, clearing intermittently for a minute or two at a time. I shall never forget recounting the story of the *Granicus* to the accompaniment of waves splashing over the bow, ejaculations of amazement from Pierre, and fog banks sweeping in across the bay. One develops a feeling of intimacy more quickly than usual on journeys such as we were making, and Pierre and I were better friends because of this unusual voyage than if we had been acquainted for years under other and more normal conditions. Before we had reached Cape Gaspé, we were both deeply under the spell of the strange, fearsome account of the unfortunate barque *Granicus*.

Captain Basile Giasson, a sealer of renown on the St. Lawrence, was the discoverer of the fate of the *Granicus*. On May 8, 1829, he was sailing just off Anticosti Island at a location then known as Belle Baie and now as Fox Bay. Since the wind was unfavorable and the ship's water supply was completely exhausted, he dropped anchor there for the night.

Coming out on deck later, he noticed a ship's boat floating on the tide, and he decided to row in and investigate. From the condition of the boat he guessed that it must have been there for months. Examining it, Captain Giasson noticed that the oars were placed neatly together and that clothing and other personal effects were scattered around the bottom of the craft. He decided to go ashore and investigate further.

A house of refuge stood on the nearby cliff, and Giasson, with three members of the crew, landed his boat and walked up toward the building. The men shouted to attract the attention of anyone who might be near, but once the echo of their voices had died away, a deathlike silence fell on the bay. The place was so lonely and dreary that the men were seized with sudden fear. They decided to go back to the ship for guns and other weapons before exploring any further.

Returning to the clearing around the house, they found

a woman's silk gown and the dress of a baby apparently about a year old. Captain Giasson picked up the garments and examined them. To his horror, he saw that they were covered with bloodstains and that both were pierced as if by stabbing.

The captain and his crew were more terrified than before. They had seen evidence of murder, and, for all they knew, whoever was responsible might be hiding in the nearby woods, ready to kill them. But Jacques Bourgeois, a stouthearted sealer who feared nothing, prevented them from running away. "We should not leave," he said. "We are armed, and if anyone tries to attack us he will get a good shower of lead."

Somewhat abashed, the other men advanced cautiously with him toward the hut, guns in hand. As they entered the outer storm door of the building, a frightful sight greeted them. More than a dozen partly dismembered human bodies were strewn on the floor or hung from beams in the ceiling!

The four men were stunned. Captain Giasson shook his head as if to clear his senses and then led the way into the inner part of the house. Reaching the center of the next room, as their eyes gradually became used to the darkness, they realized that they had left one horror to find another equally gruesome.

Above the burnt-out logs in the enormous fireplace hung two iron pots filled with human fragments. This second horror was too much for them, and they broke down and sobbed bitterly.

Finally, they steeled their nerves to explore the rest of the house. In the next room they found three trunks. Shaking with fear, the men opened the lids and found that the trunks were crammed with dismembered human bodies that had been carefully preserved with salt.

An true Accompt of all such Gold, Silver, Jewels and Merchandizes, late in the Possession of Cap.t William Kidd, which have been Seized and Secured by us under written, Pursuant to an Order from his Excellency Rich: Earle of Bellomont Cap.t Generall & Governor in Chiefe in & over his Maj.ties Provinces of y.e Massathusets Bay &c bearing date July 9.th 1699 Vizt)

	Gold Ounces	Silver Ounces	Precious Stones or Jewels
In Cap.t William Kidd's Boxes			
One Bag of 53 Silver Bars		357	
One Bag of 79 Bars Silver		442½	
One Bag of 74 Bars Silver		427	
One Enameld Silver Box gilt in which are			4 Diamonds set in a Gold Locket & one Diamond loose one large Diamond set in a Gold Ring
Found in Mr Duncan Campbell's House			
No. 1 — One Bag of Gold	58½		
2 — One Bag of	94		
3 — One Handkercheife	50		
4 — One Bag of	63		
5 — One Bag of	38½		
6 — One Bag of	19¾		
7 — One Bag of		203	
Also Twenty Dollars, one halfe one quart.r p.s of eight, Nine English Crowns, one small Barr of Silver, one Small Campesheat a Small Chaine, a Small bottle a Corral Necklace, one p.s white Stone p.s Checquered Silk			
In Cap.t William Kidd Chest, Two Silver Boxes, Two Silver Candlesticks, one Silver Porrenger & Some Small things of Silver of		82	
Rubies Small & great Sixty Seven, Green Stones two One large Loadstone			69

NEW HAVEN HISTORICAL SOCIETY

The ship in the sky off New Haven (CH. I)

RIGHT ABOVE: *Group clinging to the capsized wreck of the* Enigma (CH. XII)

RIGHT BELOW: *Lifeboat manned by a Cohasset crew, April 2, 1918* (CH. XIII

LEFT: *The wreck of the* Giovanni *at Cape Cod* (CH. XIV)

The rocks of Anticosti, where the Granicus *was wrecked* (CH. XV)

Nye, caught in the jaws of the whale (CH. XVI)

Painting on rocks off Portland Head Light marks location of the wreck of the
Anne C. McGuire (CH. XIX)

PHOTO BY FRANK KELLY

Giant waves crash over seawall in Scituate, flooding roadways and homes. (CH. XX)

PHOTO BY GEORGE DIXON

RIGHT ABOVE: *Two units of a motor inn were swept away when a storm-whipped wave at high tide crashed through a protective seawall.* (CH. XX)

PHOTO BY LABAN WHITTAKER

RIGHT BELOW: *Ice sculpture in Copley Square, Boston* (CH. XX)

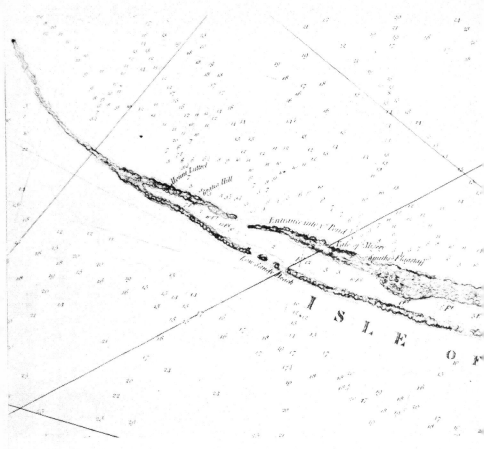

ABOVE: *A 1766 chart of Sable Island* (CH. XXII)

RIGHT: *A typical Sable Island shipwreck* (CH. XXII)

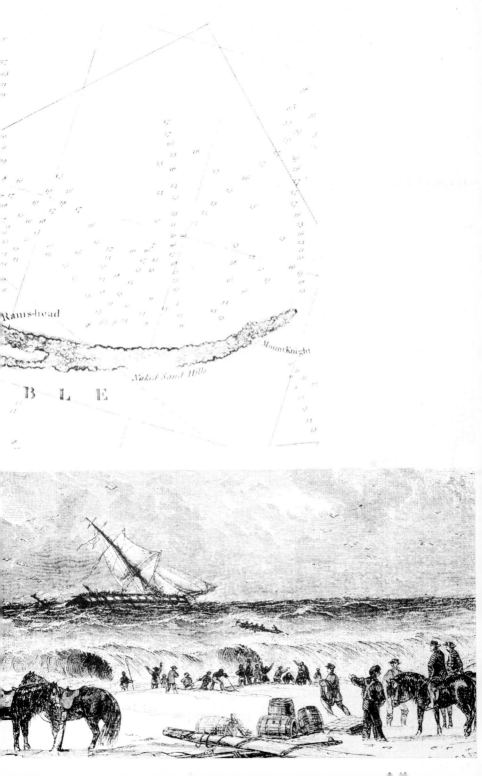

Rams-head

Mount Knight

Naked Sand Hills

B   L   E

LLOYD'S LIST
AND
SHIPPING GAZETTE.
(Established 1726.)

ALL RIGHTS OF TRANSLATION AND
REPRODUCTION ARE RESERVED.

Registered at the General Post Office as a Newspaper

*The Editorial, Advertisement & Publishing
Offices of "Lloyd's List & Shipping Gazette"
are at*

LLOYD'S, ROYAL EXCHANGE,
LONDON, E.C.3

MONDAY MAY 22 1922

TO-DAY'S SUMMARY.

SHIPPING AND COMMERCE.

The P. & O. liner *Egypt* sank off
Ushant on Saturday evening as a
result of a collision with the French
steamer *Seine*. The loss of life was
heavy.

The Egypt (CH. XXVI)

OPPOSITE LEFT: *The world learns of the* Egypt's *tragedy in Lloyd's list.*

RIGHT: *Observation chamber that allowed the Italians to recover the* Egypt's *gold*

RIGHT: *Commendatore Quaglia with gold ingots from the* Egypt (CH. XXVI)

FAR RIGHT: *Celebration on the salvage craft* Claymore, *with gold from the* Niagara

BELOW: *The* Niagara, *which went to the bottom with millions in gold* (CH. XXVI)

Captain William Kidd in cell at Boston's stone jail (CH. XXVII)

Captain Kidd's body in chains at Wapping-on-the-Thames (CH. XXVII)

In still another room they saw what they believed to be the first live person in this house of horrors. Lying in a hammock at one corner of the room, apparently asleep, was an enormous mulatto.

This man had the shoulders of a wrestler and apparently the physique of a Hercules. On the floor nearby was a pan of soup. Repressing his repugnance, Captain Giasson spoke to the man in the hammock. When there was no response, Giasson walked up to the hammock and touched the mulatto's body. The man was dead.

Continuing their search around the grounds, the group found a small outhouse. Inside was another pile of human remains, these too terrible to describe.

In all, the captain estimated there must have been twenty-four bodies in all. Although the ground was still frozen on that May 8, the master of the sealing craft decided that everything must be buried as soon as possible, and his crew set to work at once. Before they had finished, the sailors were digging by lantern light.

After the last fragment of human flesh had been covered over the crew returned to their craft for the night. The next morning, with all evidence of murder and death under ground, they began a thorough investigation.

Their most important find was a letter that obviously the mulatto had written. It was addressed to his mother, Mary Harrington of Barrick Street Cove, Liverpool, England. Anyone discovering the letter was asked to send it to his mother.

The next discovery was a ship's journal or log. Here the men read of how the *Granicus* had been wrecked, and of how Harrington had killed the others. He believed that the members of the crew would all die in any case, and that he could prolong his own life by taking theirs. He had lived to write in the log book until just a few days before the sealers arrived and landed at Anticosti.

That afternoon the sealers carried aboard their vessel six trunkloads of clothing in good condition and four other boxes of merchandise of all descriptions. They set sail that night for the Magdalen Islands and turned all their material over to Monsieur Colbach, a representative of Admiral Coffin, the Governor.

When Pierre returned me to the mainland I went at once to Quebec, where I pieced together all available information concerning the incident. I was helped by lighthouse keeper Placide Vigneau at Parrott Island, and J. M. LeMoine of Spencer Grange.

I learned that the Irish barque *Granicus* had sailed from Quebec on October 29, 1828, homeward bound with lumber for Cork.

Early in November she was caught and wrecked at East Point, Anticosti. Every person aboard reached shore safely, and when they discovered a sign directing them to a hut of refuge a few miles away, they had high hopes.

Unfortunately, vandals had ransacked the hut, and all food had been taken away by the keeper of the hut because it had spoiled. He had never brought replacements.

The captain divided the food from the *Granicus* among the twenty-five people, and the survivors lived on this for several weeks. Then one night the mulatto had carried out his terrible act, justifying himself with the excuse that all would soon die in any case.

Harrington stayed alive for weeks on his horrible diet, but as the weather grew warmer he found himself getting weaker. Finally he crawled into his hammock for the last time.

He had murdered the others sometime in February 1829,

and on April 28 he made his last entry. It is probable that he died of scurvy or poison from the decayed food.

The full details are so gruesome that I have spared the reader. The complete account is available for anyone with a lively curiosity and particularly strong nerves.

XVI

The Name of Nye

The name of Nye is an important one in the annals of American maritime history. It was Peleg Nye who fell from his whaling ship's longboat back in March 1863 and found himself in the jaws of a huge sperm whale. He was taken to the bottom by the whale and then released when the whale died. Although badly injured, he recovered in a few weeks. Years later down on Cape Cod he often showed admiring youngsters the marks on his knees from the whale's jaw.*

Then there was Captain Ebenezer F. Nye, who sailed with Captain Herbert Wight aboard the whaleship *George & Susan* in 1849. One day he and his men fastened onto a giant whale just before sunset. Determined to secure the monster, they fought for three long hours. Then, as dark-

---

* James Bartley in 1891 was swallowed by a whale and remained inside for two days, until the whale was captured and cut open, revealing the unconscious Bartley. Bartley lived for many years but said he often had severe headaches for no apparent reason. In my book *Mysteries and Adventures,* I tell the entire story.

ness threatened, the lights of the *George & Susan* vanished from the sight of the men in the whaleboat.

Fearing that Captain Wight would not find them, Nye ordered the line cut and they lost their whale. Then he lighted the lantern and placed it in the bow. Midnight passed and still there was no sign of their ship. Nye realized that the situation was very serious. When morning came and they saw only the broad expanse of the Pacific, he told the others in no uncertain terms that they were up against it. The worst fear of a whaler—being adrift on the open sea—was their fate.

"We haven't much hope of being picked up," Nye admitted to the others, "but I am going to do something about it. The Marquesas Islands are about two thousand miles from here, but they are the nearest land I know of. We can just give up and die in the sea, or we can try to reach land. Which is it to be?"

The others agreed that they should all make an effort to reach the Marquesas Islands. Nye went to work constructing a makeshift quadrant out of the glass in his compass and wood from a thwart. After a few days the only one who really believed that they had a chance to reach their goal was Ebenezer Nye. He kept at his chosen task, each day making observations and recording his findings.

On the third day supplies ran out, but a providential rain allowed the men to catch a large amount of water in the canvas sail, from which it was poured into the water kegs. Each man was given half a pint a day. Ten days later violent hunger assailed them. That afternoon a porpoise breached out of the water and actually landed in the middle of the boat. The starving crew leaped on it and tore it to pieces with knives and the boat hatchet, devouring the porpoise raw. Two days later they were without food again, and their water was used up shortly afterward.

On the fifteenth night out, one of the men, crazed by drinking sea water, leaped into the ocean to his death. The next morning another hard rainstorm gave the five survivors additional drinking water. Four days later a second man leaped to his death, followed on the twentieth night out by the third to end his life in similar fashion.

The very next day land was sighted, one of the Marquesas group, but by this time the survivors were so helpless that all they could do was to allow the whaleboat to drift ashore by itself. They were too exhausted to act. Out of water and food as well, they noticed a small pool near shore, but were unable to make the effort to approach it. Finally, Captain Nye forced himself over the side of the whaleboat down onto the shore and crawled on his hands and knees toward the pool, where he drank deeply. Then he pulled off his shoe, filled it with water, and carried it down to his comrades, who revived themselves with the liquid.

That very day natives appeared and took them to one of the larger islands, where they were nursed back to health. Eventually they reached Tahiti.

At Tahiti, Captain Nye heard for the first time about the California gold rush. Looking around the harbor he noticed a centerboard schooner of ninety tons at anchor and, upon investigation, learned that the craft was owned by a landlubber. Nye volunteered to sail her to San Francisco. Two weeks later, during Nye's watch below, the owner's carelessness caused the schooner to capsize, and three of the crew drowned.

Nye, the owner, and four sailors survived. With the vessel over on her beam ends Nye cut two flat-bottomed boats free from the deck and floated them up to the surface, after which he secured them to the hull, which remained afloat like a log.

This time Nye was determined to have enough to eat. A hole was cut in the side of the schooner, and supplies were brought out to the two flat-bottomed boats. In this manner Nye and his companions stayed alive for the next twenty-two days, when they were hailed and picked out of the boats by an English merchantman that landed them at Honolulu. Never before in recorded history had one man participated in two such remarkable sea adventures while trying to get back to his home.

In spite of a total of forty-four days at sea in open boats Captain Nye was able to sail back to New Bedford, getting there long before the *George & Susan* returned from her whaling voyage in the spring of 1852.

Our final story concerning the Nye family is about Thomas W. Nye. Why this particular Nye adventure has escaped the notice of the world is a mystery, but we may look in vain for a mention in the *World Almanac,* under Marine Disasters, of the unhappy tragedy which befell the *John Rutledge,* an American packet ship in command of Captain Alexander Kelly of Barnstable, Massachusetts.

Thomas W. Nye of Fairhaven, Massachusetts, was twenty-one years of age when he began working as a seaman on the *Rutledge,* owned by Holland and Ridgeway of New York City. After one successful voyage, he sailed to Liverpool on the vessel, and on January 16, 1856, began the return trip to New York with Captain Kelly still in command. The cargo consisted of railroad iron. There were 120 passengers, and the crew numbered 25.

The weather became very rough. Not only was a sailor lost from the jib boom, but a passenger also was swept overboard from the deck when a giant sea mounted the rail.

About noon on February 18 the *Rutledge* entered an ice field in latitude 45 degrees 56 minutes West, but then steered away from the dangerous area. The next day was foggy. The fog cleared late in the afternoon to reveal a gigantic ice field, stretching away to the east and northeast as far as the eye could see. Captain Kelly ordered the *Rutledge* to stand to the southeast, and three hours later she was clear again.

Suddenly, without warning, there was a sickening crash, and all hands rushed out to see what had happened. The ship had struck an old growler, an iceberg practically submerged, and the sharp ice had sheared off part of the *Rutledge*'s forefoot. To make matters worse, water was pouring into the craft's hold.

Desperate measures were taken to save the ship, for Captain Kelly knew that he was several hundred miles away from the nearest land, which was either Newfoundland or Nova Scotia. He ordered much of the movable cargo thrown overboard and was soon able to get at the leak. The crew stuffed pillows and clothing into the area, but apparently it did no good.

All this time both pumps were being worked at top speed, every able-bodied man on the ship taking his turn. But soon it was evident to all that their task was hopeless. There were not enough lifeboats to take everyone, but when this was learned many of the passengers announced that in any case they preferred the relative safety of the ship to a small lifeboat. Nye knew that the lifeboat was a better risk and dressed himself in plenty of underwear and two heavy suits of clothing for added warmth.

Five boats were launched. The captain sent the mate and the carpenter for a final look at the leak in the ship as his lifeboat waited alongside. While they were below, the line parted, and the mate and the carpenter were left behind to perish with the passengers. About fifty persons went down with the ship, which disappeared beneath the waves shortly afterward.

In a boat with twelve others, Nye was able to keep in touch with the captain's craft for about half an hour. Then the wind and the waves separated them, and the captain and his companions were never heard from again. Unfortunately, Nye had with him only two pounds of "Fancy" crackers and a demijohn of water. The bottle was accidentally broken and the compass was also smashed by accident. Others, however, had brought water.

On the second day out they sighted a vessel that came so close they could see she was carrying a great load of lumber. She sailed away without noticing the relatively small lifeboat.

By the end of the first day Nye came to know most of his fellow survivors. Mrs. Atkinson, one of the two women in the boat, was the wife of the first mate, and did not know that her husband had gone back aboard the *Rutledge* to perish with the ship.

The weather was bitterly cold. In the confusion of sighting another iceberg Nye fell overboard but was helped back into the lifeboat, his clothing wet and uncomfortable.

A straw was used for the sip of water which each person was entitled to take three times daily, and if anyone took a swallow instead of a sip he was deprived of his next portion when the time came. Consequently, all in the lifeboat developed a terrific thrist, and everyone except Nye resorted to drinking sea water. It was not long before the effects of this salt water became noticeable.

The first to die was the wife of a passenger, whose husband was with her in the lifeboat. When her body was thrown into the sea, a huge shark that had been following the lifeboat quickly pulled the dead woman under. Her husband perished the next day, and his body was thrown over. The shark also consumed his corpse. Two young brothers were the next to go, passing away on the seventh

day of the ordeal at sea. Their father died shortly afterward, and all three bodies were cast into the ocean, to be
devoured in turn by sharks, which by now had increased
to three in number. That night another passenger perished
and was thrown into the sea at daybreak, but strangely
enough, all three sharks had vanished.

The boatswain died on the eighth day, followed by another passenger, but it was such an effort for the weakened
survivors to throw anyone into the sea that the remaining
passengers agreed that if someone else died, the dead bodies
would stay in the lifeboat. Then came the moment when
Mrs. Atkinson, the mate's wife, told Nye that she was about
to perish.

"Please take my watch and these rings. Give them to my
husband when you see him," she said.

Nye accepted the jewely, and she died shortly afterward.
Before nightfall the three remaining survivors were also
dead, leaving Nye alone in the lifeboat with the four
corpses of his former companions.

Toward noon on the ninth day Nye sighted a vessel
sailing toward him. It was the packet ship *Germania*, but
he had no strength to wave to her. By this time his limbs
were frozen solid, and he feared that in spite of everything
he was doomed to die. He had seen other craft sail by the
lifeboat without noticing it, and reasoned that this ship
would do likewise.

However, as he watched his heart gave a leap! One of
the sails was lowered and the vessel hove to. Nye realized
that the ship was going to attempt to rescue him, and fell
into a temporary sleep. An hour later he saw a ship's boat
high on a nearby wave, and soon the boat was alongside.

"Help," he cried feebly.

The boat came nearer and one of the sailors, thinking

that he had to say something, blurted out, "What are you doing here?"

At first the seamen were so horrified at the boatload of corpses with one half-living man among them that they did not even offer assistance to Nye. Finally they recovered their senses and helped roll him over the side and pull him across to their boat. They tied Nye's boat behind theirs and started back to the *Germania*.

Taken aboard the packet, Nye at once saw Captain Wood, the *Germania*'s master. The captain could not believe this sole survivor was not closer to seventy than twenty-one in years, so old had his ordeal made him appear. Nye's normal weight of 165 pounds had dropped to seventy-five, but his mental reactions were still very acute.

The New Bedford sailor was given careful attention in the sick bay, and subjected to the remedies of the period. The first step was to immerse the legs of the sufferer in ice water, "thus avoiding the evils so frequently occurring from too-sudden exposure of frost-bitten extremities to a more elevated temperature." Captain Wood next fed the patient cayenne pepper, thus gradually exciting the heart, arteries, and nervous system. Then his extremities were covered with bran poultices. A few days later the danger of mortification was gone except for two toes, which were amputated.

On March 11 the *Germania* was hit by a hurricane that drove her back into the Gulf Stream, but she rode it out and finally sailed into New York harbor on March 24, 1856.

As soon as the news was published that Nye was the sole survivor from the wreck of the *John Rutledge*, he was besieged by relatives and friends of others aboard the ill-fated vessel. He could offer them little encouragement, and as it eventually turned out, none of his shipmates was ever heard from again. Nye's family reached New York the next day, joining him aboard the *Germania.*

On March 26 Nye was removed from the *Germania* on a litter, and carried over to Pier 11 on the North River, where he and his family went aboard the steamer *Potomski,* bound for New Bedford.

When Nye arrived in New Bedford, he was the hero of the hour because of his miraculous escape from death on the high seas. But more than six months would pass before he could walk again, and the shock to his nervous system never left him.

The experience did not frighten him away from the sea, however, as he made several voyages after his recovery. Peculiar fortune followed him. At Aspinwall, Panama, the boiler on the *Ocean Queen* exploded, killing nine men but leaving Nye unharmed. On another occasion he arrived in England at the height of a great cholera epidemic, and while others dropped dead all around him, he escaped with no sickness at all.

Later in life Thomas Nye left the sea, becoming a constable at Fairhaven, Massachusetts, where he served as a policeman until his death on June 12, 1905. He was remembered for two things by those who knew him best. First, that he was the sole survivor of the iceberg shipwreck of the *John Rutledge.* Second, that until his death he carried with him in a tiny box the three relics of the terrible disaster at sea that Mrs. Atkinson had given him in the lifeboat—the two rings and a watch.

XVII

The Crime of Ansell Nickerson

During the summer of 1971, while doing extensive research around Chatham, Massachusetts, I was introduced to a young lady who taught school in the region.

She was planning a play about the weird, unhappy career of Ansell Nickerson, a young resident of Cape Cod who was either a clever murderer or a misunderstood victim of the high seas.

The teacher told me where the remains of Ansell Nickerson were supposedly buried. Not only would she take me to the cemetery where his tombstone could be found, but she promised to invite me to the school play written by her about the incident. I never heard from her again, and I never have found Ansell Nickerson's grave.

Early one Sunday morning in November 1772 Ansell Nickerson was alone on the schooner *Abigail* off Cape Cod. There had been a gale around midnight, but when the *Abigail* was sighted by another Cape Codder, the storm had passed.

Joseph Doane was sailing from Chatham to Boston when

he sighted the *Abigail*. While still off the "back side" of the Cape, at about ten o'clock that morning, he noticed a flag of distress flying from a vessel offshore.

Figuring that the weather must have been worse out to sea because of the flag fluttering from the schooner, he brought his own craft alongside and rowed across in his jolly boat. Seeing that the other schooner was the *Abigail,* also out of Chatham, he went aboard to search for the crew.

Captain Doane found but one survivor aboard, twenty-three-year-old Ansell Nickerson. Nickerson appeared terribly frightened, and not because of the storm. He had a story to tell, an account so weird that a Boston newspaper later stated that it was "the most surprising . . . in this, and perhaps any other Age of the World."

Ansell Nickerson claimed that on Saturday he was aboard the *Abigail* with four other Chatham men, namely Captain Thomas Nickerson, twenty-seven; Sparrow Nickerson, twenty-nine; Elisha Newcomb, twenty-seven; and William Kent, thirteen. With the exception of Kent, the others were related. Thomas Nickerson and Sparrow were brothers, Elisha had married their sister, and Ansell was first cousin to the brothers.

The schooner had left Boston that same Saturday, and had on board something which was very precious to Ansell. He had invested his savings for the last three years in a giant cask of Jamaica rum, which was carefully chocked on deck.

Around two o'clock the following morning, according to Ansell, the lights of a topsail schooner came into view, and then he noticed flares in four small boats from the schooner which were approaching the *Abigail*. Ansell, now wide awake, did not like the situation, fearing that the boat might be filled with British sailors, members of a boarding party to impress Yankee seamen.

Ansell was known as a "New Country Whig with Rebell notions," to quote the Boston *News-Letter,* and was willing to take any risks to avoid impressment. He made sure that he had a good grip on the taffrail on the side away from the four boats, and when the visitors came aboard he let himself down carefully, until his feet touched "the Moulding under the Cabin Windows."

Clinging to his perch, Ansell listened as the British marines located first one and then another of the crew. He heard shouts and then screams as his fellow Cape Codders were aroused and attacked. The noise of scuffling became louder. Then he heard three distinct splashes which he feared were the three Cape Cod men being tossed into the sea to their death. Later Ansell thought he could hear the screams of the Kent lad as the boy was transferred to one of the small boats. Still later there was a noise as though the cask of rum was being rolled along the deck, and then the boarders sounded as though they were toasting each other with Ansell's hard-earned liquor. This angered him almost to the point of climbing back up on deck and remonstrating with the boarders, but he finally decided that if he did so he would be overpowered and probably killed. And so he waited.

Time went by, and the sounds of revelry continued. As he clung to the taffrail, another thought struck Ansell. Possibly the sailors were pirates, and not British seamen at all! Maybe they planned to take over the schooner, and he would eventually be captured.

Shortly afterward he heard a group of men enter the cabin, after which there was a debate among the boarders as to whether or not the *Abigail* should be burned. Finally the group agreed to a hasty departure without destroying the craft. Then there was silence.

Ten minutes later the lights of the four boats were seen

leaving the *Abigail,* and the regular strokes of the oars were clearly heard.

Waiting for a short time, Ansell pulled himself up on deck. He was alone on the schooner. All the others had vanished! His search revealed many things, however—blood on the deck planking, the money chests smashed and rifled, and his precious, costly cask of rum broken into and robbed of all but a few meager gallons.

In despair he called for the others, but there was no answer. Now in panic, he ran below, grabbed a distress signal and hoisted it high on the mast. He set the wheel and lashed it. Then, as the first gray streaks of dawn appeared in the eastern sky, he gave way to despair and stood leaning against the taffrail, staring at the distant shore.

When Captain Doane sighted the *Abigail,* as later stated by Governor Thomas Hutchinson, she was then between Chatham "and the island of Nantucket." Captain Doane saw that there was "much blood upon deck, and traces of blood which had run at the scuppers, and marks of plunder, by broken boxes, stove casks," and other indications of violence.

The captain was able to pilot the *Abigail* into Chatham Harbor. Ansell was soon examined by Squire Edward Bacon, the Barnstable magistrate, and then was taken to the mothers of William Kent and of Thomas and Sparrow Nickerson to inform them of the tragedy. When he repeated the story to the bereaved wife of Elisha Newcomb, she was overwhelmed, and never fully recovered from the shock.

The whole affair was too much for Justice Bacon, who wrote everything that he had discovered about the case to Governor Thomas Hutchinson at the Province House in Boston. Hutchinson also was staggered at the possibilities. Had a British press crew taken all the men from the *Abi-*

at the same time as the *Wadena,* was still on the shoal. On board were Captain Andrew Welsh, master; Captain Benjamin Mallows, marine underwriter; and Captain Elmer F. Mayo, of Chatham, in charge of wrecking operations. The *Fitzpatrick* lay quite a distance from the *Wadena,* and those on board did not see the Life-Saving boat when it went out, as they were busy putting down hatches. The men on the *Fitzpatrick* had just started their steam pump when Captain Mayo glanced over the port rail and saw a capsized boat with four men clinging to it. At first he thought it was one of his own wrecking boats. Then he recalled that two or three hours earlier, before the weather shut in, he had observed a signal of distress flying on the *Wadena.* He now decided that the capsized boat belonged to the Life-Saving station.

The lifeboat was slowly drifting toward the *Fitzpatrick,* and Mayo quickly threw overboard a large wooden fender, hoping it might find its way to the shipwrecked men. It did not, and meanwhile three of the four survivors had slid off the capsized boat to perish in the sea.

Mayo now astonished his shipmates with the declaration that he would go to the rescue with the barge's dory. Totally unfit for so perilous an enterprise, the dory was only twelve feet long. It had capsized two days before and lost both the tholepins and oars at that time.

Two pieces of pine wood, a serving stick, and an old rasp were quickly driven in for tholepins, and two old sawed-off oars were obtained. In this crippled condition the little dory was lowered over the rail and took the water right side up. Mayo threw off his boots and oil jacket, strapped a life-preserver about him, and went over the side into the dory.

Watching his chance, Mayo began to row with skill and judgment as he swept across the heaviest line of breakers.

He then located his man, sighting him half-concealed through the mist and spray that was rapidly obscuring the entire area. Mayo pulled ahead with all his might. Ellis later explained that he waved his hand toward the *Fitzpatrick* after Rogers drowned and saw a dory thrown over the side, but after that, on account of the high waves and mist, he saw nothing "until all at once the dory hove in sight." Captain Mayo rowed close alongside the capsized boat, and as he did so, Ellis reached out and dragged himself into the dory.

Mayo's work was so far well and bravely done, but the most dangerous part of the rescue effort was still ahead. Mayo could not pull back to the barge, nor would he be able to reach the shore on the inside of the point. He had to make his landing on the outside where the surf was most dangerous.

Then he noticed a man coming down the beach who would soon reach a position on the shore right across from his craft.

The man on the shore was Francisco Bloomer, a veteran surfman. As soon as Bloomer was abreast of the boat, Mayo drove it forward with great power. Caught by a towering breaker, Mayo steered as best he could. Bloomer ran into the surf and grabbed the gunnel. The boat filled, but Bloomer soon had both men above the wash of the sea. An hour later Mayo and Ellis were recovering at the Monomoy Life-Saving Station.

When Captain Mayo left the *Fitzpatrick* on his mission of humanity, he was warned that he would never live to accomplish it. When it was done and tidings of it spread abroad, it was proclaimed a noble and brilliant achievement.

In recognition of Mayo's extraordinary feat of daring, the Secretary of the Treasury, Leslie M. Shaw, bestowed upon him the gold Life-Saving medal, which may be awarded only to those who display the most extreme and heroic daring in saving life from the perils of the sea. Surfman Ellis was likewise honored and promoted to keeper of his Monomoy station.

Without question, there was no more skillful or fearless crew on the whole coast than the one that set out to save the men of the *Wadena,* and since it appeared that the *Wadena* remained safe for days after the disaster, there was a general conviction that the men were practically a sacrifice—on the one hand to the unfortunate panic of the men from the barge, and on the other to their own high sense of duty, which would not permit them to turn their backs on a signal of distress.

In the words of the Life-Savers of old and the Coast Guardsmen of today, their motto should never be forgotten: "We must go out; we don't have to come back."

XIX

Wrecks around Portland, Maine

ANNE C. MAGUIRE (GOLDEN STATE)

Captain Thomas O'Neil was terribly worried. He had started his voyage aboard the recently converted *Anne C. Maguire* some time before sailing out of Buenos Aires in ballast. His destination was Quebec, but off Casco Bay, in the vicinity of Halfway Rock, he had been caught in a blizzard. Sailing in by Alden's Rock, he believed he had a safe course for Portland Inner Harbor, but in this he was wrong.

Until this fateful Christmas Eve in December 1886 the clipper ship *Anne C. Maguire* had had a glorious history. She had been launched on January 10, 1853, with part of her cargo already aboard. Originally christened *Golden State,* she was a beautiful craft with very fine lines, her ends long and sharp.*

---

* Built in the shipyard of Jacob A. Westervelt at New York, she was 188 feet long, 39.8 feet in beam, and her depth of hold was 21.6 feet. By old measurements she was 1363 tons, by new measurements 944 tons.

On her first voyage her master was Captain L. F. Doty. Leaving New York on February 8, 1853, on her third day at sea she fell in with the *Northern Crown*. Eight hours later the *Crown* was so far back she was soon lost over the horizon. The very next day the *Golden State* passed the clipper *Ariel* and left her completely out of sight to leeward in a short space of time.

The luck of the *Golden State* changed, however, when she was 10 days out. On February 17 she had gone 327 miles under royals, but on the very next night all three topmasts went overboard with everything attached, and Captain Doty was forced to put her into Rio.

After repairs had been completed, she sailed from Rio on April 6 and reached San Francisco 97 days out.

Her second voyage was made under Captain Andrew Barstow. The *Golden State* left New York on May 25, 1854, arriving at San Francisco on September 28, in 125 days. She had fallen to leeward of St. Roque and lost a week in beating around. She reached a point within 700 miles of the Golden Gate in 14 days from the line, but had light winds and calms the rest of the way.*

While near Cape Horn, in heavy gales, Barstow had seen the clipper *Golden West*, under single-reefed topsails, also bound in the same direction. The ships crossed the line in the Pacific the same day, the *State* three degrees to the eastward of her competitor, thereby gaining better trades and arriving in San Francisco four days ahead of the *Golden West*.

The third voyage was between New York and China. The *State* went out to Hong Kong in 90 days and returned in 105 days from Foo Chow. The fourth voyage was over

---

* O. T. Howe and F. C. Matthews, *American Clipper Ships*, p. 242.

the same route, 114 days on the outward passage and 95 days on the return.

Captain Henry L. Hepburn then took command of the *Golden State*. Leaving New York on March 19, 1857, he was 93 days to Hong Kong and also 93 days from Foo Chow to New York. On the homeward run she was 31½ days from Java Head to the Cape, a time that was beaten later only by the *Challenge*. The *State* was 74 days from Anjer to port.

On her next voyage mutiny broke out on board. On the outward passage to Hong Kong, when off Penang, the crew refused duty on the plea that the food was insufficient. The mutineers attacked the officers and boatswain with hand-spikes and escaped in boats to Penang, where they were taken into custody. The first mate died of his wounds.

After arrival at Hong Kong, the *Golden State* made a voyage to Bangkok, followed by one to Australia. On this latter outward passage, she reached Sydney in a leaky condition, the crew and even the passengers having been compelled to pump day and night to keep her afloat.

Captain Charles E. Ranlett now took command of the *Golden State*. He had a light-weather passage of 128 days from New York to San Francisco, and then took 94 days to reach Cork, Ireland. Her cargo of wheat was 1195 short tons, which was considerably under her original register capability. After crossing from Liverpool to New York in 20 days, in ballast, she again loaded for San Francisco, going out in 120 days in light winds.

She now changed masters. Under command of Captain Rowland T. Delano, the *Golden State* sailed from New York to San Francisco in 121 days, arriving on July 6, 1863. Later she loaded guano at the Chincha Islands for Hamburg. Seventy-one days out she was in 25° North, 37° West, a good run thus far. Eight days later, in a heavy gale, the decks were swept by a giant comber and the mate and two men were washed overboard to their deaths.

Then came the period when the *Golden State* was confined to trade between New York, China, and Japan. She always was a favorite and had the longest career of any vessel ever so engaged in her particular type of activity.

In May 1867 it was stated that her cargo of tea, recently imported, was the largest ever received at New York and that it had been sold prior to arrival for $1,000,000. Leaving New York in June 1867, she went out to Hong Kong, Amoy, Hong Kong again, and arrived back at New York in under eight months on the journey, including all detentions. On November 22, 1872, she reached San Francisco in 34 days from Shanghai, a very fast run.

In 1873–74 Captain John C. Berry was in command, Captain Delano having remained ashore in Fairhaven, Massachusetts. Captain Berry was in command when the *Golden State* took her last departure from New York as an American ship, on January 13, 1883. Then bark rigged, she sprang a bad leak in the North Atlantic in very stormy weather and in March put into Rio in distress. Her cargo was discharged and she was sold to D. & J. Maguire of Quebec, who renamed her *Anne C. Maguire* and put her under the Argentine flag. She was operated in the Atlantic trade until December 1886 when the craft approached Portland and disaster.

Watchers awaiting her on shore saw the *Maguire* making her perilous way just off the ledges near Portland Head Light. Joshua Strout, who was then keeper, did everything in his power to signal the captain to keep off but to no avail. She piled high and dry on the rocks, a dreary wreck.

There were fifteen crewmen on board besides Captain Thomas O'Neil, his wife, and his young son, Thomas, Jr. Joseph Strout, the son of Joshua, immediately saw their plight. By good seamanship the Strouts got a line to the ship as quickly as possible. A boatswain chair with snatch block was fixed up and the crew, together with the captain and his family, were taken ashore one by one.

Let us ask Robert Thayer Sterling, a keeper of Portland Head Light after the time of the Strouts, to tell us what happened:

"There have been stories told about the wreck of the *Anne C. Maguire* but this is as I got it from Captain Strout before he passed away. She was of British register, her owners being in Quebec. They had failed, and in order that the creditors might gain something out of it they deemed it wise to place an attachment on her when she arrived in American waters. The sheriff's department had notified Captain Strout to be on the watch for her a week before she arrived, so everybody around the lighthouse had been keeping a vigilant watch. None suspected that she would sail right into their backyard.

"After the crew had come ashore, and all was safe and sound, two men from the sheriff's department served the attachment. The Captain's sea chest was opened and the ship's papers handed over. A very interesting thing happened while the Captain was hunting for his papers. His money that he kept in his long billfold was gone. What had become of it? As soon as everything had quieted down he spoke to his wife about it. She assured him that the big roll of bills was safe in her bandbox, for she had had the presence of mind, just before being taken off from the ship, to go to the sea chest and take care of the money, for no one could tell what might happen. She always carried the bandbox when going ashore so she had that with her when she arrived at the lightkeeper's dwelling.

"This was Christmas Eve, and as soon as the sheriff got back to Portland it did not take long for the news to spread and Christmas Day found many relic seekers out at the lighthouse. It was said that the ship carried a heavy insurance."

With a blizzard sweeping Portland Harbor and the entire coast the *Anne C. Maguire* went to pieces in a few days.

The ship's crew remained with Captain Strout for several days until the business was settled. Then the crew was discharged and sent home by the British vice-counsel.

Painted letters on a black wall of pointed cliffs commemorate the perils and rescues of that fateful Christmas Eve. Captain Strout and his sons were hailed as heroes by those who witnessed the rescue. Each summer thousands walk to the edge of the shore and read the inscription. The writing, telling of the wreck, is renewed every few years so that it is as fresh today as it was the day it was first painted.

THE WRECK OF THE *WENDELL BURPEE*

In several of my books I mention Cape Elizabeth, its lighthouses, and the shipwrecks of the immediate vicinity.

I had heard rumors of the *Burpee* wreck at Broad Cove around the turn of the century, but until last summer, when Charles Wood was able to give me details of the disaster that befell the schooner, the story of what really happened had remained a mystery.

The schooner *Wendell Burpee* sailed from Port Liberty, New York, on March 26, 1901. She was bound for St. John, carrying a cargo of 153 tons of soft coal and having on board a crew of four men, including the master. Three days after her departure she touched at Hyannisport, Massachusetts, and remained there for a week because of unfavorable easterly weather.

On April 6, the wind being fair from the southwest, sail was again set and she proceeded on her course. About noon the wind shifted to the south, and later into the southeast with driving rain. After dark, sail was shortened and the northeast course was maintained until about midnight, when the wind becoming stronger, the mainsail was taken in.

On the morning of the seventh the gale was so heavy that the standing jib carried away and the captain decided to heave to with her head offshore. Half an hour later he sighted land and made out two lighthouses. At first he supposed they were the twin lights of Matinicus Rock.

It was soon discovered that the land was Cape Elizabeth, and the captain decided to make an effort to run into Portland Harbor. The weather at that time was rainy and misty, while a heavy surf and undertow, due largely to a high sea on the previous day, had hit the area.

Because of the high seas, the Life-Saving crew of the Cape Elizabeth Station were exercising careful vigilance by patrolling the shores north and south of the station, as was the custom during the day when the weather was thick.

About ten-thirty that morning the south patrolman, Surfman Parker, reported to the station that a vessel was in sight to the eastward. It was soon identified as a schooner, some three miles away. She was under a reefed foresail, and later was identified as the *Burpee.*

The schooner was standing to the southward and the seas were sweeping her decks. While the keeper was watching her with his glass, she suddenly stood off, jibbed her foresail, and headed northward toward Portland Harbor. Notwithstanding that she was obviously making heavy weather of it, she now had a fair wind, and the Life-Saving men did not consider her in any special danger. They believed that she would succeed in making Portland Harbor without disaster, especially as she showed no sign of distress and did not ask for assistance.

Before long, however, it was observed that her crew were making efforts to set the mainsail, and as they succeeded in hoisting it only partway up, the keeper was satisfied that they were having trouble managing the vessel, which carried no headsail.

She was now approaching Trundy's Reef, a dangerous ledge that projects some distance into the sea, and the onlookers feared she would not weather it.

Keeper Dyer now promptly summoned all his crew and proceeded with the utmost haste for the north boathouse, which is located about two miles from the station, and the schooner was kept in sight by the surfmen every moment until they reached the woods on the north side of Broad Cove, when she was still standing to the northward. As they emerged on the other side of the woods, however, it was noticed that she had come to an anchor inside Broad Cove Rock, which is about three fourths of a mile from the shore.

Thirty minutes had been consumed by the Life-Savers in reaching the boathouse. There was very small chance of launching the surfboat in the heavy seas, and the keeper, therefore, ordered the beach cart manned, and with the aid of a number of outsiders, who eagerly volunteered their services, the Life-Savers hastened back for Trundy's Point.

The vessel was in view again just before the point was reached, and the Life-Savers observed that her anchor chain had parted and she was drifting helplessly, stern foremost, into Broad Cove.

Continuing as fast as they could, the Life-Savers now were impeded somewhat by having to clear a way through a stone fence for a passage for the apparatus. Finally arriving at the northern edge of the cove, the Life-Saving men and volunteers met the son of the lighthouse keeper at Cape Elizabeth. He gave them the unhappy news that the crew had attempted to leave the schooner in their small boat, the craft had capsized, and all but one of them had been drowned.

The sole survivor was Mate John Swenson, who succeeded in swimming ashore and had been taken to a cottage nearby, where he was quickly given the necessary stimulants and supplied with dry clothing. He recovered rapidly and was able to walk to the station, where he appeared to suffer no ill effects from his experience.

Shortly after dawn the following day, April 9, Surfman Alexander discovered the body of the cook, George S. Forester, who was from St. John, New Brunswick. The bodies of the other two, Captain Lewis Merseburg of St. John, and Charles Kindon, sailor, of England, were never recovered.

Considerable criticism was aimed at the Life-Savers for the tragedy, causing Lieutenant Ross, who inquired into the circumstances, to make a signed statement which should cover the situation.

"The foregoing account proves, I think, that the life-saving crew did everything in their power to assist the *Wendell Burpee*. The evidence shows that the keeper used good judgment in proceeding to the north boathouse, for it is in that vicinity that all on shore supposed the craft would strike in case she failed to weather the land.

"The place where the schooner struck is about $1\frac{1}{8}$ miles north of the station, and the testimony of competent witnesses places her about 75 yards from high-water mark. She remained in good condition, and, therefore, it is obvious that no difficulty would have been experienced in rescuing the entire crew with the breeches-buoy apparatus had they stood by her even for a few minutes instead of rashly trying to escape in the yawl.

"The testimony of the mate who survived is clear to this point. He says that while the crew were trying to put more sail, the schooner kept drifting nearer the shore and in the emergency the starboard anchor was let go, but the cable almost instantly parting the port anchor was resorted to. That, however, held on only a few moments, and the vessel being at the mercy of the wind and the sea soon stranded, the breakers sweeping over her from stem to stern and tearing the deck house in pieces.

"Two sailors hastily took to the rigging, but to all on board it seemed that the craft could not many minutes withstand the shock of the sea, and with this fear uppermost in their minds all hands determined to abandon her. No sooner had the yawl cleared the schooner, however, than it capsized, and the occupants were thrown into the seething surf, only Swenson, the mate, reaching the shore alive."

XX
⚓

The Hurricane of 1972

The gale that began on Friday, February 18, 1972, developed into one of the worst hurricanes since the steamer *Portland* went down in 1898. In the 1898 storm, almost three quarters of a century ago, the entire mouth of the North River, which separates Scituate from Marshfield, was scoured out in a gigantic furrow two and a half miles north of its original site.

Patrolman George M. Fallon, who has lived in Scituate all his life, agreed with me that a return to the 1898 mouth of the North River would have been probable if the 1972 storm had kept up two hours more.

At low tide on February 19 Patrolman Fallon actually stood in the sand in the old mouth of the river, some two miles south of the present opening. He estimated that the beach was dug out at least six feet in depth.

"I have never seen anything like this," Fallon said as he returned from a survey of the area.

The Maine coast also was buffeted by the gale. Two keepers at lonely beacons out to sea there were having their

troubles. Officer-in-charge Stephen Garsznski at Boon Island Light, ten miles from Cape Neddick Light, with his
assistant Garth Clough, had a harrowing experience.

At the height of the storm Garsznski was afraid that the
lighthouse itself was in peril.

"The ocean was swirling around in the kitchen, filling it
with kelp, seaweed, and rocks. Three buildings were badly
battered.

"We lost one wall of the boathouse, almost every window in the main house was broken in, doors were blasted
open and the latches broken.

"Two doors protecting the entrance to the all-important
generator room were smashed open by the heavy seas and
the electrical generators ruined.

"We lost one window when the storm started, and we
patched it. Then all power went out at 2:30 P.M.

"Just before that I headed for the room with the radio
to report to the mainland. As I entered the room a wave
surged right across the island and broke through the window over the radio. It never worked again.

"Our windows kept smashing one by one after that,"
concluded Garsznski.

The two men were taken off by a helicopter that landed
on the copter pad on this isolated island.

At Halfway Rock Light, in Outer Casco Bay off Portland, Maine, Keeper Frank Reese recalls thirty- and forty-
foot breakers buffeting the island. One breaker tore away
the lighthouse fuel tank, which vanished in the sea.

"When we lost that fuel tank, we lost everything. You
see, everything on the light is electrically operated—the
light, the heat, everything. No fuel, no generator to make
electricity.

"We lost the wood walkway, that's sort of a porch around

the light, and part of the boat ramp which we use to land personnel and supplies.

"I tried the phone several times during the afternoon after we lost our power at 3 P.M., but it was dead. I couldn't get anything.

"Then during the evening I picked it up again, mostly because there just wasn't much else to do. This time it worked. I told the base what the situation was and that we were all right, although it was cold," said Reese.

The outdoor temperatures at Halfway Rock stood between 18 and 22 degrees during the night. Inside the lighthouse it dropped from 72, where it was before the storm, to 38 by morning.

The Halfway Rock crew was taken by helicopter from the ruined lighthouse station.

All mariners were notified immediately by standard radio transmissions that both Boon Island and Halfway Rock were worthless as navigation beacons until repaired.

Eastern states from Maine to the Carolinas shivered in the grip of a howling winter storm that dumped as much as twenty inches of snow on some areas and lashed others with sleet and rain.

Along the shores of Massachusetts Bay conditions were serious. Flood tides breached sea walls and poured over low-lying North and South Shore areas, including Revere, Marblehead, Winthrop, Scituate, and Hull. Hundreds were driven from their homes.

In upstate New York several cities reported accumulations of more than a foot of snow. A number of basketball games and many other public events were called off.

Winds gusting up to gale force buffeted Pennsylvania, and snow more than twenty inches deep blanketed some areas in the western mountains. Philadelphia was drenched by a mixture of rain, sleet, and snow.

Roads in some sections were made virtually impassable by ice. Near Boone, North Carolina, traffic was backed up for six miles on a road to a ski resort, and wreckers did a thriving business pulling cars out of roadside ditches.

"They're backed up from Boscoe Plum into Sugar Mountain and Beech Mountain," said Highway Patrol dispatcher Jim Cannon. "They just come up here with straight-tread tires and try to go on, and they can't do it."

Many rural roads were blocked by snow. Main highways were passable in most cases, although some were closed for stretches as long as twenty-five miles. Icy roads caused at least three deaths, two in North Carolina and one in Massachusetts.

Gale-warning flags were flying as far south as Virginia, and freezing temperatures were forecast for Florida, although that state escaped the main impact of the storm.

All in all, the area hardest hit was New England, where blinding snow and gale-force winds caused coastal flooding and power failures and brought transportation to a virtual standstill.

PART III **GOLD**

XXI

Le Chameau

In 1725 a mighty French warship, heavily laden with treasure, sank in a terrible gale at Cape Breton Island in Canada. Her name was *Le Chameau*. Twenty-five years ago I began research on the details of this marine disaster which took place along the rocky Atlantic shores of this Maritime Province.

Two days after the disaster Commissaire Ordonnateur DeMezy at Louisburg agreed that the gale had been the worst in the thirty-five years he had been on or near the sea.* Because of the intensity of the storm off Nova Scotia, "not even a pig came ashore alive." DeMezy learned that all along the coast from Grand Lorambec to Baleine the beaches were strewn with wreckage. In the midst of the debris he discovered a beautiful figurehead that he recognized as having come from the shattered *Le Chameau*.

The French transport *Le Chameau* had been caught in

* Evidently the storm was not wide in scope, as neither Sidney Perley in his *Historic Storms* of 1891 nor Ivan Ray Tannehill in his *Hurricanes,* written in 1938, mentions it.

a violent northeast gale that reached its height on the night of August 25, forcing the coastal inhabitants inland. At ten o'clock the following morning when they dared to return, the residents found the shore littered with debris from what had been a terrible disaster.

Several fragments of wreckage were identified as coming from *Le Chameau,* and soon all officials of the area converged at the shore, for there had been many very prominent passengers aboard the warship, as well as a cargo of gold and silver coins.

It is probable that the shipwreck occurred without warning, for most of the bodies washed ashore were dressed in nightclothes. Among the 310 members of the ship's company, all of whom drowned, were Monsieur de Chazel, the new intendant of Canada; Monsieur de Louvigny, the new governor of Trois Rivières; and the son of De Ramesay, late governor of Montreal.

In 1949 I called at many homes on the island of Cape Breton, and then visited the general area of Chameau Rock, the boulder marking the legendary spot where *Le Chameau* first hit on her journey to disaster and death. I knew that through the years many divers had explored the bottom in attempting to bring up the gold of *Le Chameau,* but the nearest anyone had ever come to profiting by their efforts was long before I reached the scene. During the summer of 1927 divers made special efforts to locate a treasure chest. Caught in the flukes of a fisherman's anchor, the chest had come to the surface for a split second and then descended to the bottom again.

After learning what I could from the older men of the area, I went down at low tide some distance from what is still known as Chameau Rock. My diving outfit was of the most primitive type, with the suit brought together by twisting the edges of the open front and tying them together into a rosette at the chest.*

In my diving I reached about forty feet, but that was my limit. The only tangible things I saw at that depth were large and small masses of sea cement, the result of rusted metal uniting with the salt water. These were so covered with the accumulation of centuries that I can only guess what they were. As events later proved, on that occasion I was within a few rods of gold and silver coins amounting in value to several hundred thousands of dollars which were brought up by Alex Storm in 1965. The only real relic from the *Chameau* that I brought up was a cannon ball, which I still have.

In two books I tell of my visit to the area of Chameau Rock, *Secrets of the North Atlantic Islands* (1950), † and *True Tales of Buried Treasure* (1951). In both volumes I give the history of the shipwreck, and mention the approximate original wealth of the treasure lost. Actually, my estimates were far too modest for today's values. I wrote that the coins were valued at 289,696 livres, or in the estimates of almost two and a half centuries ago, about $160,000. However, certain individual coins from the wreck, when eventually auctioned off, brought twelve to twenty times their original value! The first ambitious diver to search for *Le Chameau* explored the bottom in 1725 just a few weeks after the ship was lost. This early diver was sent down wearing nothing but grease smeared over his body. The man chose to try for gold at Kelp Cove where 150 bodies had come ashore immediately after the storm.

---

* I used the identical suit in diving over the atomic scientist's yacht *Trani* when it was recovered from the bottom two miles out to sea from the beach at Duxbury, Massachusetts, in 1958. See *Mysterious Tales of the New England Coast*, opposite p. 86.

† At the time of the publication of *Secrets*, Alex Storm was only twelve years old.

He was joined in the next few weeks by more than a dozen others, all with their naked bodies smeared with grease. There are various reports as to just what they brought up to the surface, but officially, these men who went to the bottom in freezing water never discovered a single coin of any denomination.

This early activity awakened the desire of scores of other divers. Through more than two centuries, generation after generation of treasure seekers continued the underwater explorations begun in 1725. Although several cannon balls were found on the bottom, nothing else was recovered, according to tradition.

In 1961, however, Alex Storm discovered one of *Le Chameau*'s cannon while he was hunting for another shipwreck. Near the cannon he found a treasure coin, the first, it is believed, ever to be brought up from *Le Chameau*. Of course, it fascinated him.

Storm eagerly made plans to dive again. Then five men visited him and said, "Hands off," explaining that the area already had been leased to them by the license they held, a permit issued by the Receiver of Wrecks in the area.* The men explained that in Cape Breton anyone planning to dive for sunken hulks must get permission in advance and that they still held the rights.

Sometime later that year Storm and the five men came to an agreement, and the six continued as partners. Actually, according to Storm, the others abandoned the search in the year 1962, making the original agreement invalid. Storm speaks of the last dive of 1961 as exciting while it lasted but fruitless in results.

Between 1961 and 1964 Storm began to work in a rebuilding project at the famed Louisburg fortification, and

---

* The men were Willard Dillon, Hyman Goldberg, Joseph Nearing, Ronald Blunden, and Robert D. MacDonald.

he also married. He never forgot *Le Chameau*, however, and eventually applied for a license to seek the gold on the French shipwreck of 1725. The permit was granted with the proviso that Storm give ten per cent of what he recovered to the province. Later the Federal Department of Transportation told him that he could keep whatever he salvaged from *Le Chameau* and would not have to give the Receiver of Wrecks anything!

And so it was that in March 1965 Storm decided to work with two new men, David MacEachern and Harvey MacLeod. The former was a successful scuba diver, while the latter had much experience in sailing. However, in March the water off Cape Breton Island is too cold for scuba divers even with wet suits, which retain some of the body temperature. So the hopeful treasure seekers decided to await warmer water.

Later in 1965, while diving about seventy feet down and within three thousand feet of Chameau Rock itself, Storm discovered ballast stones on the bottom arranged in such a fashion that he realized they must be from *Le Chameau*. For more than two centuries the stones had kept a precious secret, seventy feet from the surface.

Elated, Storm redoubled his efforts. After hours of strenuous work he and his two partners found artifacts which included a gold watch, silver dining utensils, and ten silver coins! *

On Wednesday, September 22, 1965, the three men began concentrated work. They sailed out of Little Lorraine Harbor, where they had been keeping their craft, the *Marilyn B. II*. Reaching the scene of the 1725 disaster,

---

* Borden Clarke of the Old Authors Farm in Morrisburg, Ontario, knowing my interest in *Le Chameau*, has been keeping me informed through the years. Because of this outstanding rare-book dealer's desire to help me, I first heard about Alex Storm and learned of the interest he had taken in *Le Chameau*.

MacLeod stayed aboard while Storm and MacEachern went over the side with their diving equipment. There they found an underwater buoy that Storm had placed at the time of their earlier descent.

The men soon discovered two more cannon. Then came a deliriously happy moment. Locating a treasure chest, which might have been the same chest the fishermen had brought up and lost again in 1927, they found it contained gold and silver!

Hopefully, the two men had taken canvas bags down to the bottom with them that day. They now paused momentarily, shook hands, and then methodically began to fill the bags with silver and gold coins. Indeed it was a great moment in their lives, one never to be forgotten. Half an hour later they rose to the surface where they overwhelmed their partner MacLeod with the canvas bags filled with treasure!

For the next twenty days they brought up bag after bag of gold and silver, bothered only by visits of lobsters which in size and number were truly unbelievable. Every lobster in the area apparently wanted to see what was going on. Late each day the gold was surreptitiously smuggled ashore and concealed until dusk. Then the wealth was taken up into the third-floor apartment of Alex Storm, where it was counted, and later taken to the bank.

Evidently the news of their discovery leaked out, because somtime later Storm's original partners appeared to announce that they were entitled to part of the treasure. By then the hoard had been transferred to the vaults of two Sydney banks, but Robert D. MacDonald of Glace Bay obtained a court injunction demanding that Storm, MacEachern, and MacLeod hand the treasure over to Sheriff James MacKillop.

Of course Storm admitted that he had signed an agreement in 1961, but he was sure that the agreement had elapsed when the others quit. Awaiting a decision of the court, Sheriff MacKillop viewed the treasure and announced that there were about a thousand gold coins and eight thousand silver coins.

Several years went by, during which time matters were at a standstill. Then, on September 8, 1970, almost five years to the day after finding the first of the treasure, Alex Storm and his two companions were notified by the Appeal Division of the Nova Scotia Supreme Court that they had won their case. The Court set aside MacDonald's injunction, and Storm, MacEachern, and MacLeod were free to claim the gold and silver. Sheriff MacKillop said that he would deliver it to the three men in three days, and he was true to his word.

The decision was appealed to the Supreme Court of Canada, and on June 28, 1971, that court ruled that the treasure of *Le Chameau* should be divided seventy-five per cent and twenty-five per cent. The seventy-five per cent would go to those who found the treasure, Storm and his two aides, while twenty-five percent would be split among the original five divers, who found nothing.

It is quite possible that eventually a million dollars will be realized from the sale of the gold, silver, and other valuable material from *Le Chameau,* so each one of the eight divers is assured of receiving a substantial amount.

Arrangements eventually were made to auction off the coins in New York. The firm of Parke-Bernet Galleries was chosen for the sale, and in December 1971, hundreds of the coins and artifacts were sold for $199,680.

According to the New York *Times,* French buyers dominated the auction, with 705 items disposed of. The sale included an emerald ring, a gold cross, silverware, fragments of a sword, and a silver watch which was in "surprisingly good condition." The day's top price was for the emerald ring, which sold for $4750. A silver coin brought $1100. Minted at Dijon in 1724, just a year before *Le Chameau* went to the bottom, it won out by $100 over another coin bought by an unidentified Frenchman. That was a nickel-sized Louis d'Or, minted at Troyes in 1723. Many gold coins, estimated before the sale to be worth $175 each, brought an average of $400 a piece.

When the auction came to a close, Alex Storm stated in an interview that he was very happy and that it had been a wonderful sale.

Incidentally, while Storm awaited the decision on the gold and silver, he and his two partners had gone down to the bottom off Scatari, searching for H.M.S. *Feversham,* which, according to Joseph N. Gores, went down in that area. In his book *Marine Salvage,** Gores tells the reader of how the Storm group in 1968 discovered a thirty-six-gun galleon that had foundered on the way to Louisburg. Locating the strong box, the drivers discovered some extremely rare Dutch daalders, the only ones of that particular type still in existence. Gores tells his readers that they also found a rare American coin, whose estimated value is $5000.

Thus Alex Storm joins the magical number of treasure finders who have salvaged from the sea the equivalent of a million dollars. The list includes Teddy Tucker, Kip Wagner, Robert Marx, Harry Cox, and William Phips.

---

* I am grateful to Joseph Gores, who has written the best book I have read on the subject of salvage, in which he mentions one of my own publications.

XXII

Sable Island

Blinding raindrops pelted against the cockpit windshield of our plane, slithered in neat little rows along its surface, and flipped off into space. Through the steel gray atmosphere of the storm we could see seven hundred feet below us the breaking crests of giant waves. The mighty Atlantic was putting on a spectacular show.

With any sort of luck, an airplane can fly through or around a rain-laden gale without mishap. But our task was far more difficult.

We wanted to find Sable Island, a narrow stretch of sand bar 150 miles off the coast of Nova Scotia, known as the Graveyard of the North Atlantic.

Unless we could bore through the fog, mist, and rain almost directly above the island, we might miss it entirely.

We were getting more discouraged by the minute. My two companions, Ray Hylan and Jerry Fund, had left with me the day before from the airport at Marshfield, Massachusetts, full of hope and confidence. We had been promised good weather but now were being buffeted by a substantial storm.

Try as we would we couldn't catch even a glimpse of our destination. With our gas being used up, we finally decided to quit and return. But the gale was just testing us, for as we headed toward Nova Scotia, the rain let up. A short time later we saw the sand dunes and the breaking waves below us.

Losing altitude, we banked sharply and made a perfect landing on Lake Wallace. We had reached our goal.

It was in 1944, while with a group sailing down Boston Bay, that I first met anyone who had ever been to Sable Island. At the moment I had been telling the listeners stories concerning gold taken from the sea and from caches on lonely islands.

I told of Phips, bringing the million dollars' worth of Spanish gold from the galleon sunk in the year 1687, of the millions brought up from the *Egypt,* and of the weird tale of Oak Island. When I had finished, one of the men spoke up:

"Well, I don't know about Oak Island or Governor Phips, but when I was ashore at Sable Island several years ago we almost dug up a great treasure. We had trouble, though, and had to abandon our plans."

"What was your trouble?" I asked.

"The sand kept sliding in and the wind filled in our excavation every time we left it," he told me. "We had a terrible time and, as we were digging late at night without the knowledge of the superintendent of the island, we finally gave it up in despair. But we had nearly reached a great hoard of money—of that I am sure—and it is still up there."

Without question the hoard *is* still there, for the men

never went back. The story so fascinated me that at my first opportunity I visited the Harvard library to study material on Nova Scotia. Several books included references to Sable Island, and one or two gave detailed descriptions of this mysterious island so far off the coast of Nova Scotia itself. But still I wasn't satisfied with what I found. The more I learned, the more I wanted to know. Finally, off to Nova Scotia I went—by air, in order to save time. By visiting Halifax and its libraries and by interviewing former residents, I pieced together Sable Island's strange history.

Sable Island is part of a gigantic sand bank—one of a series that exist in the area between New York and New-foundland. Included in the group are Nantucket Shoals, George's Bank, Brown's Bank, La Have Bank, Sambro Bank, Emerald Bank, Sable Island Bank, Middle Ground, Canso Bank, Misaine Bank, Banquereau Bank, St. Pierre Bank, Green Banks, and the Grand Banks of Newfound-land. Each bank extends for from fifteen to three hundred miles and each is made of particles of pebbles, coral, shells, and sand. The water over them is usually no deeper than seventy fathoms. Of the fourteen, only one is above the high-water mark: Sable Island.

Sable Island Bank is one of the largest; the bank itself is two hundred miles in length from east to west and about ninety miles in breadth. The highest part of this dangerous navigational hazard is Sable Island itself. Running from east to west, it is twenty-five miles long and barely two miles wide at its broadest part, in North Latitude 44 degrees and in West Longitude 60 degrees. When seen from the air, it appears to form two parallel sandy ridges, curved slightly with the bulge at the south, giving the shape of a bow or new moon. Between the ridges is a valley containing two salt-water lakes.

The island is made dangerous by its deceptive color, which seems to change to match the water. The luckless mariner finds himself hopelessly stranded on a reef before he realizes the proximity of the island. It is comparatively low, no part of it being more than a hundred feet above the sea. From West Point on the island a bar stretches westerly for about twelve miles and is dry for two miles in ordinary weather. Then, for ten miles more, the sea breaks over it almost continually. Cross seas ripple its surface even on the calmest days. At the eastern end of the island a similar condition exists so that, although in length the island is only about twenty-five miles from end to end, in stormy weather it presents a hazard of ugly breakers fifty miles long!

Three bars surround the island—the inner bar, middle bar, and outer bar. These bars, of course, are much more dangerous than the island proper. If a vessel hits the island, a line can be shot out from shore to the survivors and those on board stand a good chance of being saved by breeches-buoy or lifeboat. But if a wreck occurs beyond either the eastern or western extremity of the island, it is almost impossible to effect a rescue.

Then, too, the sides of the bars are very steep, with thirty fathoms of water on the north and 170 fathoms on the south, so that a vessel can easily scrape her bottom out and sink in deep water a moment later. The whole catastrophe might conceivably occur in less than five minutes. Sometimes, after a heavy gale or a thick fog, the only signs that such a tragedy has actually taken place are a body or two and some wreckage that float ashore. For the 250-odd known wrecks of Sable Island, an equal number have sunk there without revealing their identity.

The sudden storms of Sable Island are described by

Simon D. MacDonald, who wrote about their peculiar characteristics in the year 1882:

"The sun often rises clear, giving indications of continued good weather, and with the exception of the sea breaking high on the bars, and the fretful moan of the surf as it breaks along the shore, there is no premonition of the coming storm. Suddenly a dull, leaden haze obscures the sun, clouds gather from all directions. The sky assumes a wild, unusual appearance. The wind begins to rise in fitful gusts, carrying swirls of sand before it. The darkness increases as the low, driving scud shuts in all distant objects. Now the gale bursts in awful fury, whipping off the summits of the hummocks, carrying before it a cloud of blinding sanddrift. Darkness adds to the horror of the scene, while the rains descend in a perfect deluge. No human voice can be heard above the tempest. The crinkled lightning for an instant lights up the mad waves, as they rear and leap on the beach. Then a sudden calm ensues. A few short gusts at first break this period of tranquility and in a few minutes the hurricane bursts again from the opposite quarter. The darkness is still intense, relieved only by the red glare of the lightning, which is quickly followed by the crashing of the thunder, as it strives to be heard above the howling blast. Gradually the storm ceases, the clouds break and pack away in dense black masses to leeward, and the sea alone retains its wild tumult."

And now for the early history of Sable Island. We cannot say positively that John Cabot sighted the island on his voyage of 1497; he only mentions the fact that he passed two islands. He might have mistaken the sand hills on Sable Island for two separate islands—but we can't prove it. In 1505 a Portuguese pilot named Pedro Reinel identified the island as Santa Cruz. Later, in 1521, John Fagundez was given the island of Santa Cruz by the King

of Portugal, as Fagundez had sighted it on a previous voy-
age. Sebastian Cabot's *Mappemonde* in 1544 includes Santa
Cruz, while in 1548 Castaldi of Italy calls it *Isolla del
Arena.*

The first mention of the island as *Sable* was in 1546
when the Portuguese mapmaker Joannes Freire named it
I. de Sable—Island of Sand.

Early in the sixteenth century, therefore, Sable Island
was well known to the cartographers of the world. We can
be positive that it was equally well known to the fishermen
and traders from the Old World. Lescarbot tells us that
the Baron de Lery, when his American colony of 1518
failed, sailed back to France and left his cattle ashore on
Sable Island.

Other early Sable Island history includes the fact that
in 1633 Mr. John Rose of Boston was shipwrecked at Sable
Island in the *Mary and Jane.* Making a small sailboat from
the timbers of the wreck, he sailed to the mainland of
Nova Scotia, only to be captured by the French, who forced
him to sail back to the island with them. At the time, Rose
reported, there were eight hundred cattle and many black
foxes roving the island. Finally he was released to return
to Boston.

Two years later America's first foreign trader, Thomas
Graves of Lynn, Massachusetts, landed at Sable Island in
the *Rebecca,* hunting for the great sea horse or walrus that
had been seen there. The expedition was a failure, however.

John Winthrop of Boston was definitely interested in
Sable Island, and I offer excerpts from his journal:

1635
June 24.] Mr. Graves, in the *James,* and Mr. Hodges, in the
Rebecka, set sail for the Isle of Sable for sea-horse (which are

there in great number) and wild cows. Mr. John Rose, being cast ashore there in the [*Mary and Jane*] two years since, and making a small pinnace of the wreck of his ship, sailed thence to the French upon the main, being thirty leagues off, by whom he was detained prisoner, and forced to pilot them to the island, where they had great store of sea-horse teeth, and cattle, and store [of] black foxes; and they left seventeen men upon the island to inhabit it. The island is thirty miles long, two miles broad in most places, a mere sand, yet full of fresh water in ponds, etc. He saw about eight hundred cattle, small and great, all red, and the largest he ever saw, and many foxes, whereof some perfect black. There is no wood upon it, but store of wild peas and flags by the ponds, and grass. In the middle of it is a pond of salt water, ten miles long, full of plaice, soles, etc. The company, which went now, carried twelve landmen, two mastiffs, a house, and a shallop.

1635

August 26.] They returned from their voyage. They found there upon the island sixteen Frenchmen, who had wintered there, and built a little fort, and had killed some black foxes. They had killed also many of the cattle, so as they found not above one hundred and forty, and but two or three calves. They could kill but few sea-horse, by reason they were forced to travel so far in the sand as they were too weak to stick them, and they came away at such time as they used to go up highest to eat green peas. The winter there is very cold, and the snow above knee deep.

1637

August 31.] Twenty men went in a pinnace to kill sea horse at the Isle of Sable, and after six weeks returned home, and could not find the island; but, after another month, viz., about the [*blank*] of September, they set forth again with more skilful seamen, with intent to stay there all winter.

1639

June 4.] About this time our people came from Isle Sable. A bark went for them, on the 2 of the 1 month, but by foul weather she was wrecked there, and of her ruins they made a small one, wherein they returned. It was found to be a great error to send thither before the middle of the 2 month. They had gotten store of seal oil and skins, and some horse teeth and black fox skins; but the loss of the vessel, etc., overthrew the hope of the design.

1641

August 21.] This summer the merchants of Boston set out a vessel again to the Isle of Sable, with 12 men, to stay there a year. They sent again in the 8th month, and in three weeks the vessel returned and brought home 400 pair of sea horse teeth, which were esteemed worth £300, and left all the men well, and 12 ton of oil and many skins, which they could not bring away, being put from the island in a storm.

1642

June 8.] About this time the adventurers to the Isle of Sable fetched off their men and goods all safe. The oil, teeth, seal and horse hides, and some black fox skins, came to near £1500.

Shortly afterward the French settlers in Acadia took all the cattle off the island to breed them ashore.

In 1738 the Reverend Andrew Le Mercier, pastor of the French Huguenot Church of Boston, petitioned for the ownership of Sable Island, receiving it in a grant some time afterward. Two years later vandals went ashore there and removed much of Le Mercier's stock and material.

In 1753 Le Mercier placed a notice in the local Boston *Weekly News-Letter* offering the island for sale and describing its advantages. In his advertisement Le Mercier said that the Island was twenty-eight miles long and ten thousand acres in size. It had no flies, he claimed, and produced twenty types of berries. Turnips grew there seven pounds in weight; rye and wheat produced thirteen bushels an acre. At the time Le Mercier had ninety sheep, thirty horses, forty cows, and forty hogs on the island. He brought his notice to a close with the following statement:

"If any person wishes to purchase the island I must know their mind within two or three months, that the crew now upon the island may be disposed of accordingly." History is silent as to whether or not Le Mercier found a buyer.

The next recorded event occurred in 1760 when Thomas Hancock (uncle of John Hancock) fitted out a schooner to carry horses, cows, sheep, goats, and hogs to the island for the benefit of shipwrecked mariners. The many wild horses still there today are believed to be descended from the Hancock strain of 1760.

It is evident that during the sixteenth century the island was much larger than at the present time—possibly fifty miles in length—and the grass growing on the sandy shores probably attracted those who wished to find good grazing for their cattle. In early times, without question, the island contained an adequate harbor, for Joseph Frederick Wallet Des Barres, who drew a map of Sable Island for his survey of the Atlantic Coast in 1766, indicated the entrance to the harbor on his chart. Years later, so the story is told, a violent storm closed the entrance, trapping two American vessels that had sought shelter there.

The oldest resident ghost on the island is that of a Paris gentleman whose wife was unjustly sentenced to the Bastille by Henry IV of France. The poor woman had attracted the attention of the king and had resisted his advances so successfully that at last he sent her off to prison. When Count de La Roche planned to make a settlement at the lonely island in 1598, he chose her from among the prisoners at the Bastille as one of the settlers. Suffering from the exposed life at Sable Island, she soon died. Later when her husband heard of her horrible fate, he passed away of a broken heart. There are those who say that whenever a French vessel is wrecked at Sable Island, his ghost appears to the survivors and files a complaint with them against Henry IV for banishing his wife to the Bastille and then allowing her to be sent to the island.

The second earliest ghost settler is that of the Regicide, one of the men who condemned Charles I to death in 1649. When Charles II ascended the throne, the Regicide was forced to escape from England and he chose Sable Island for his exile, dying there around 1680. Every May 29, the anniversary of Charles II's return from exile, this Roundhead gentleman puts on his broad-brimmed hat and appears at night to the islanders. He sings psalms through his nose so loudly that, even if there is a strong gale, he can be heard all over the island above the roar of the wind and waves. At least, that's the story!

The most famous phantom of all is the ghost of the Lady with the Missing Finger, a beautiful woman who was aboard a vessel wrecked at the island many years ago. According to the legend, several parts of which are contradicted by history, the ship *Princess Amelia* sailed from England to Nova Scotia with furniture, supplies, and two hundred passengers. The people were to help settle Nova Scotia under Prince Edward, later known as the Duke of Kent. He also became the father of the future Queen Victoria.

After stopping for more supplies at Halifax, the *Amelia* was caught in the grasp of a terrible storm and wrecked at Sable Island. All on board except a Mrs. Copeland were drowned. She had somehow managed to clutch a hatch cover and drift ashore.

Unfortunately for Mrs. Copeland, at that time there was a group of wreckers—little better than pirates—living on Sable Island. The head of one of the families, the worst villain of them all, had watched Mrs. Copeland drifting ashore on the wreckage and was down on the beach waiting for her. Rushing out into the surf, he dragged her off the hatch cover and up above the wash of the sea. About to carry her into his home and bring her back to consciousness, he noticed a beautiful emerald ring on her left hand. Whatever good intentions he might have had vanished when the costly stone caught his eye, and without any hesitation he tried to pull it from the ring finger of her left hand. But the immersion and battering in the salt water had swollen her fingers, and the ring remained firm. The pirate decided that he would be forced to choke Mrs. Copeland to death, after which he would hack off the finger with the ring on it. This he did, then with the finger and ring in his pocket, he hurried home to show his wife and family the horrible prize.

"No good will come of this," shouted his wife, and she fled from the house. Visibly stricken by what he had done, the wrecker sold out his rights on the island and moved to Cape Breton, where he settled on the Salmon River. But he later fell upon hard times and pawned his emerald for twenty shillings.

The people of Nova Scotia and Cape Breton gradually became suspicious of the wreckers of Sable Island, especially when trinkets, rings, and other expensive ornaments were brought ashore to be sold. More and more personal articles of great value turned up in different towns and cities on the mainland. Finally, in his capacity as Governor of Nova Scotia, Prince Edward of England decided to take action himself. He dispatched his most trustworthy mariner, Captain Edmund Torrens, to the island for an investigation. Leaving Halifax aboard the brig *Harriot,* the captain ran into a gale that wrecked him on the very island for which he was sailing, and all but Torrens and a dog drowned.

After building a makeshift shelter and burying the dead along the shore, Captain Torrens made plans to survey the island. One day he started out with his dog in the direction of the eastern end of Sable Island, more than twenty miles away. It was a beautiful day with high, fast-moving clouds overhead. Torrens, although temporarily marooned on an island far out in the ocean, decided to make the best of it. By late afternoon he had hiked down to the very eastern tip. When he turned to face the west, a gorgeous sunset greeted him, and he stood in awe of it. It was a view he never forgot—the entire island spread out before him, bathed in red from the last rays of the setting sun—and he paused until the beauty had faded from the sky.

As the final tinge of color vanished, a faint rustling breeze awakened him to the fact that he was miles from the end of the island where the shelter had been erected. Sable Island was a dangerous place at night, with giant rats, quicksand, sea lions, walruses, and countless other perils awaiting him. With a start he realized that he could not reach the tent which he had erected at the other end of the island before nightfall. Striking inland, he walked rapidly.

The wind increased, and soon was whistling through the beach peas and the coarse marsh grass, rising in intensity as the night approached. Captain Torrens was filled with a sense of dread. As he looked into the fading sunset little could be seen except the contours of the giant sand dunes, interspersed with broken wreckage from several century-old galleons cast high and dry by the storms.

Suddenly he saw ahead of him a weird-looking building, resembling at the same time a small barn and a hut. He noticed the outline of a chimney above the gabled roof, and hurried toward the promise of shelter. As he approached the hut, his dog became badly and inexplicably frightened, refusing to follow. Nevertheless, the captain threw open the door and went inside. There was a fireplace, and in a short time he had built a warm fire with bits of driftwood gathered near the hut. He then brought in enough hay to make a comfortable bed. Still restless and uneasy, however, he took a walk out near the lake, his dog following reluctantly.

Finally, as Torrens returned to the hut, the dog began to bark furiously. The captain saw nothing out of the way and entered the hut. To his amazement, there was a lady sitting by the fire frantically trying to dry her long, dripping hair. Her face was pale as death. Her only garment was the torn fragment of a costly gown which was badly stained with blood, dirt, and sand. Her eyes, which seemed to implore Torrens to help her, followed him closely as he strode around the room.

"Good heavens, madam," exclaimed the bewildered captain, "who are you, and where did you come from?"

But she did not answer. She held up her pale white arm, and its wetness glistened in the flickering firelight. With her right hand, she pointed to the fingers of her left. Her ring finger was missing—only the stump remained. Blood from the wound ran down her arm, the drops hitting the dirt floor one at a time.

Having salvaged some medical supplies from the wreck, Captain Torrens hastened to tell the woman that he would obtain bandages and attend to her mutilated hand. Suddenly she slipped around him and fled into the night.

Torrens was afraid that her experience had driven the woman insane. He hurried after her, but she had disappeared. Terribly curious and perplexed by the whole affair, the captain returned to his tent in the morning, but the following night again started for the hut, leaving his dog in the tent at the eastern end of the island.

Reaching the hut, he rebuilt the fire, then, as on the previous night, went out for a stroll. On his return he found the Lady with the Missing Finger sitting by the fireplace. She recognized him at once, and he walked closer. Suddenly he remembered her as a woman he had met in Halifax, the wife of Dr. Copeland, the surgeon of the 7th Regiment.

"Why, Mrs. Copeland, is that you?"

She bowed her head and showed him the bloody stump of her finger again.

"What is it you wish?" he asked her. "How can I help you?"

She again pointed to the mutilated hand.

"I understand now," cried the captain. "You were murdered for the sake of your ring!"

She bowed her head in solemn agreement.

"Then I'll track the villain down wherever he is," shouted the captain. But at this she shook her head, indicating that she was not interested in vengeance.

"Well, then, what can I do for you?" he asked. "Perhaps you wish me to find the ring and restore it to your family? Is that it?"

She nodded her head vigorously.

"Then I promise you that I'll do everything possible to recover the ring," said the captain.

The Lady with the Missing Finger smiled, bowed her head, and, beckoning him aside, she slipped out of the door. He never saw her again.

Shortly afterward Captain Torrens and his dog were rescued from the island. Three months later he obtained his first clue to the mystery of the stolen ring: the wrecker whom he suspected of guilt was living near the Salmon River on Cape Breton Island. Arriving at the man's home, the captain found that the wrecker had gone to Labrador. His family, however, invited Torrens to come in. Soon he became well acquainted, and one night sat down to dinner with the family.

Back in Halifax, and with just such an occasion in mind, the captain had purchased a cheap but gaudy ring. Now he appeared at dinner wearing the flashy ornament. It attracted immediate attention, and the young daughter of the house could hardly wait until the meal ended to examine it.

"Why, Captain Torrens, your ring is beautiful! But it isn't half as pretty as the ring Daddy took off the lady's hand at the island."

"Be still, child," shouted the angry mother. Then, remembering her guest, she lowered her voice and said, "Your father got that ring from a Frenchman who found it on the sand there." And the mother walked over behind Torrens so that she could signal the child to agree.

"Oh, that's all right," said Torrens easily. "Never mind how he obtained it. I am a collector of rings. If it is as pretty as you say, would you let me see it?"

"No, we can't show it," said the mother. "My husband turned it in at a watchmaker's shop in Halifax for a twenty shilling advance."

"Oh, well, it doesn't matter," Torrens said, and he changed the subject at once.

The next day he left for Halifax. Taking two of his lieutenants with him, he started out early in the morning on his strange quest. Luckily, there were only two watchmakers in all Halifax at that time, and he found the ring in the first shop.

"An old Sable Island wrecker brought in that ring," said the watchmaker, visibly impressed by the seriousness of the captain and his two lieutenants. "But I have merely advanced him twenty shillings on it and the value, as you know, is many times that price."

"Of course, I realize that," said Torrens. "However, let me hold it." The watchmaker handed the ring to the captain.

"Now," said the captain, "I have searched five months for this ring, and I know its entire story. Here are the twenty shillings which you advanced. If the owner wants more, tell him to bring you the finger that was cut off to get the ring!" Leaving the watchmaker speechless, Torrens walked out of the shop with the emerald safely tucked away in his wallet.

Shortly afterward Torrens was transferred to another part of the British Empire, and the subsequent history of the ring is unknown. But every few years, so it is said, the ghost of Mrs. Copeland, the Lady with the Missing Finger, returns to Sable Island.

The gold from the *Princess Amelia* must still be inside the strong box of the craft, and a conservative estimate would be half a million, as the vessel was on the way to Prince Edward's Island to lay the groundwork for the new government there. The payment was aboard.

With five hundred other shipwrecks on or off the island, several millions more in treasure must lie not too far off-shore.

There have been so many wrecks at Sable Island that an entire book could be written about them. A few outstanding ones include *Skidby, Puritan, Rafaele, Cora May, Farto, Britannia, Bridget Ann, Nerito, Gladstone, Ironsides, William Bennett, Star of Hope, East Boston, Adonis, Vampire, Growler, Hannah, Industry, Trafalgar, Francis, Albatross, Ruby, Wyoming, Lord Bury, Amelia Foch, Valkyrie, Charles H. Taylor, Golden Bow, Silverwings, Crofton Hall, Weathergage, Alpheus,* and the *Independence Hall.*

To discuss just one of the wrecks, here is the story of the

ship *Arcadia* of Warren, Maine, which hit Sable Island on November 26, 1854, with 147 passengers and a load of glass, lead, iron, and silks.

Sometime earlier Dorothea Dix, a pioneer in aiding the insane, learned that lunatics had been sent to Sable Island because there were no institutions ashore for them. Traveling to the island in 1853, she heard that the three lunatics who had been there had finally left. During her stay on the island, Miss Dix witnessed one shipwreck, that of the schooner *Guide,* during which the captain had temporarily gone raving mad. When she returned to the United States she turned her attention to obtaining several suitable surf-boats for the islanders to man in rescues. Miss Dix wrote to Captain Robert Bennet Forbes of the Massachusetts Humane Society and to other groups. As a result four fine metal lifeboats were sent to Sable Island.

On November 27, 1854, one of the new metal lifeboats, *Reliance,* was pressed into service in the rescue of eighty persons from the *Arcadia.* Darkness fell before the remaining passengers could be brought ashore. Superintendent M. D. McKenna ordered the lifeboat to make no more trips for the night. In his journal he recorded the unhappy scenes:

"When night came on, and we had to haul up our boat, the cries from those left on the boat were truly heartrending. In the hurry of work, families had been separated, and when those on shore heard the cries of those on the wreck at seeing the boat hauled up, a scene was witnessed that may be imagined but cannot be described."

Superintendent McKenna was worried that with the rising wind the ship would not last the night. When dawn came he was happy to see her still out in the surf. By ten o'clock that morning, the entire ship's company of 168 had been safely landed. Within a few hours the *Arcadia* went to pieces.

In 1953, six years after my first visit, I returned to Sable Island, again by plane, leaving seven hundred books for the lighthouse keepers and coast guardsmen to read. I was greatly impressed by the herd of wild horses that was galloping along the shore when we landed. I remember hundreds and hundreds of seals as well. They were startled when we flew over them, and headed as fast as they could for the relative security of the ocean.

On this second trip I learned of many events of 1926, for that was an exciting year on the island. A nineteen-year-old horse died, a half keg of liquor washed ashore, and one island inhabitant left for Halifax in a hurry. The crop for that year had been sixty bushels of potatoes, thirty barrels of turnips, twenty bushels of carrots, ten bushels of beets, and five bushels of parsnips. The cabbage crop, however, had been a failure.*

The one inhabitant who left the island in 1926 was the cook, McGowan by name, who took one of the island dories and sailed away. He was picked up and eventually landed on the mainland. To this day no one knows why he left the island.

In 1971 scuba divers visited the island but were unsuccessful in their attempt to get gold from a treasure galleon said to be offshore. Bruno Matas and Raymond Potvin, both of Lawrence, Massachusetts, went to Sable Island in the summer of 1971, and returned with many fascinating relics.

Another event of 1971 was the visit of the Mobil Oil-Tetco group. The company has revealed that there are a

---

* I later learned that during good years strawberries on Sable Island grow as large as golf balls.

number of zones containing natural gas condensate and crude oil on the island.

On my last visit to Sable Island I climbed to the crest of a great hummock of sand. Standing there, I looked far out toward the east. I thought of Sable Island's experience with the ocean. Slowly it moves eastward. I wondered if it would ever reach the edge of the shoals, stand tottering on the brink of the abyss, and then plunge forever into the depths. I believe, however, that there will always be a Sable Island.

XXIII

The Gold Hoax

I almost hesitate to include this chapter on "A Notable Lawsuit, Summarized by Franklin H. Head." The reason is that regardless of how many times I state that the following tale is not true and actually is merely an interesting but pleasant hoax, it has been incorrectly accepted as the truth by almost everyone who has read it since 1894, when it was written.

In 1931 *Forum* Magazine copied it, and although *Forum* made it clear that it was a hoax, thousands of people still were convinced it was not.

One of the summer visitors to Deer Isle, Maine, in the 1890s was Frederick Law Olmsted, the older of the two landscape architects by that name. There at Deer Isle he met Franklin H. Head of Chicago. To amuse the Olmsted family, Head wrote the "Notable Lawsuit" story.

A copy was sent to me by my father-in-law, the late Louis Vernon Haegg. I repeat, the story you are about to read is not a true account, but simply an amusing hoax.

A NOTABLE LAWSUIT
SUMMARIZED BY FRANKLIN H. HEAD

The suit commenced some three years since by Mr. Frederick Law Olmsted against the various members of the Astor family, in the New York Superior Court, attracted considerable attention at the time, both from the prominence of the parties to the litigation and the large amount claimed by Mr. Olmsted, something over $5,000,-000. The case has not yet come to a hearing, owing to the delays at law; the matter has, in a measure, passed from notice, scarcely anything connected with it having appeared in the newspapers.

Through the courtesy of Mr. Olmsted, I spent several days as a guest at his summer residence on Deer Isle, which lies in Penobscot Bay off the mouth of the Penobscot River, on the coast of Maine; and having heard in detail the history of the cause of action, which seemed to me to prove the maxim that truth is stranger than fiction, I take pleasure in recounting the story as told me by Mr. Olmsted and the members of his family.

An ancestor of Mr. Olmsted, seven generations back, whose name was Cotton Mather Olmsted, was an Indian trader and spent a part of each year, from 1696 to 1705, in what is now the State of Maine. His treatment of the Indians was always fair and honorable, whereby he won their confidence and esteem. Winnepesaukee, then the head sachem of the Penobscot tribe, was at one time severely wounded by a bear, and because Mr. Olmsted cared for him, dressed his wounds and aided greatly in his recovery, the chief, as a token of gratitude, presented him with Deer Isle, before named, a portion of which has ever since remained in the possession of his descendants, and is now the property and summer residence of Mr. Frederick Law Olmsted. The original deed of gift, written on a piece of birch bark, and bearing the date of January 24, 1699, is still in the possession of Mr. Olmsted. After the independence of the United States was acknowledged, the validity of the transfer was recognized and affirmed, and a formal patent issued by the secretary of the Treasury during the second term of President Washington's administration.

Upon the rocky shore near the residence of Mr. Olmsted, and to the extreme south end of the island, is a cave, the opening of which is on the sea. The cave is about ten feet wide and ten feet high, of irregular shape, and extends back into the rock formation some twenty-five feet. It has evidently been excavated by the ceaseless action of the waves upon a portion of the rock somewhat softer than its surroundings. At high tide the entire cave is under water, but at low tide it can be entered dry-shod, being entirely above the sea level. The bottom of the cave is covered with coarse sand, five or six inches deep, below which is a compact bed of hard blue clay. At low tide the cave is often visited by the family of Mr. Olmsted and the other residents of the island. On one such visit Mr. Olmsted observed upon the rock at the inner end of the cave some marks or indentations, something in the form of a rude cross, which seemed to him possibly of artificial origin. If so, it was of ancient date, as its edges were not well-defined—were rounded and worn, as by action of the waves and ice. Still, it appeared more regular in form than the other markings upon the walls of the cave, and one day when in the cave, Mr. Olmsted suggested to his family that as stories of Captain Kidd's buried treasures had sometimes located them upon the Maine coast, they should dig at the place below the cross for such hidden wealth.

Purely as a matter of sport, the excavation was commenced; the sand was cleared away, and to their surprise, a rectangular hole in the clay was discovered, about fifteen by thirty inches on the surface and about fifteen inches deep. This was filled with sand, and when the sand had been carefully removed, there, plainly to be seen upon the bottom of the hole, were the marks of a row of boltheads some three or four inches apart, and extending around the bottom about one inch from its edge. The appearance was precisely as if an iron box heavily bolted at its joints had been buried on the compact clay, and after its removal, the excavation having been filled with sand, the impression had been permanently preserved. After a perfect fascimile of the bottom of the hole had been taken in plaster of Paris, the excavation was again filled with sand. The clay was so hard that the taking of the cast did not in the least mar its surface. As there were various legends relative to the presence of Captain Kidd upon the Maine coast, the discovery of the excavation was sufficient to awaken eager interest in the question of the iron box and the person who had carried it away.

About the year 1801, a French-Canadian named Jacques Cartier, who was one of the employees of John Jacob Astor in his fur trade, and who had for several winters traded with the Indians and hunters along the upper waters of the Penobscot River, returned from New York, where he had gone to deliver the season's collection of furs, and expressed a desire to purchase from Oliver Cromwell Olmsted, who was then the owner, by inheritance, of Deer Isle, either the whole island or the south end, where the cave before described was located. Mr. Olmsted refused both requests, but finally sold him a few acres near the center of the island, where Cartier built a log house and lived for many years with an Indian wife, hunting and fishing occasionally as a diversion, but giving up entirely his former method of gaining a livelihood. This trader had for several years previous to 1801 camped upon the south end of Deer Isle when collecting his furs, passing up the Penobscot River and its tributaries in a small canoe, and storing his furs in a hut at his camping place until the end of his season, when he sailed with his little cargo for New York.

He had always been extremely poor, having but a meager salary from Mr. Astor; but when he purchased a portion of the island, he seemed to have an abundance of money, sufficient in fact to meet his wants for many years.

Occasionally, when under the influence of whiskey, he would speak vaguely of some sudden good fortune which had befallen him; but when sober he always denied ever having made the statement, and seemed much disturbed when asked about the source of his wealth; this led to various suspicions among the few inhabitants of the island as to the honesty of his methods in acquiring it.

These suspicions ultimately became so pointed that Cartier suddenly disappeared from the island and never returned. On searching his cabin, some fragments of paper were found, torn and partially burned, so that no connected meaning could be determined from them. On one fragment was the signature of John Jacob Astor, and on another, in the same handwriting, the words: "absolute secrecy must be observed because . . ."

These fragments were preserved, however, and are now in the possession of Mr. Frederick Law Olmsted. From the story of the trader and from the fragmentary papers, Mr. Olmsted fancied that there might be some connection between the mysterious box and the newly acquired wealth of the trader, and that the secret, if there was one, was shared by Mr. Astor.

As the trader for many years previous to his sudden good fortune had camped upon the end of the island immediately adjoining the cave, it might readily be conceived that a heavy storm had washed the sand away so as to make the top of the box visible, and that he had found it and taken it with him to New York to Mr. Astor, with his boatload of furs. His desire to purchase this particular location on the island harmonized with this suggestion.

Various questions presented themselves regarding this theory. Had the box contained the long-lost treasures of Captain Kidd? If so, to whom did the box and its contents belong? Mr. William M. Evarts, to whom Mr. Olmsted applied for an opinion as to the legal phase of this question, after careful examination of the evidence, gave his views, in substance, as follows:

1. That Captain Kidd, in the year 1700, had acquired by pillage vast treasures of gold and gems which he had somewhere concealed prior to his execution in 1701.

2. That if such treasure was concealed upon Deer Isle, that island was the absolute property, at that time, of Cotton Mather Olmsted; for while the record title to the island bore date in President Washington's administration, in 1794, yet this, as appeared by its tenor, was in affirmation of the title made in 1699, at the time the island was given to Cotton Mather Olmsted by the Indian Chief, Winnepesaukee, and established the ownership of the island in Mr. Olmsted when the box, if concealed by Captain Kidd, was buried; and that Frederick Law Olmsted, by inheritance and purchase, had acquired all the rights originally held by his ancestor in that part of the island where the treasure was concealed.

3. That, as owner of such real estate, the treasure would belong to him, as affixed to the land, as against the whole world, except possibly the lineal descendants of Captain Kidd, if any there were.

Mr. Olmsted learned that in his early life Mr. Astor kept

for many years his first and only bank account with the Manhattan Bank, and as the books of the bank are all preserved, he was enabled, by a plausible pretext, to secure an examination of Mr. Astor's financial transactions from the beginning. His idea in this search was to learn if Mr. Astor's fortune had increased at the same time as that of the French-Canadian.

The business of both Mr. Astor and the bank was small in those early days, and the entries of the customers' accounts were much more in detail than in our time, when, as a rule, only accounts are recorded. The account commenced in 1798, being one of the first accounts opened after the picturesque organization of the bank by Aaron Burr, and for several years the total deposits for an entire year did not exceed $4,000. Mr. Astor shipped some of his furs abroad, and others were sold to dealers and manufacturers, and whenever he drew on a customer with the bill of lading, the books of the bank showed virtually the whole transaction. Entries like the following are of frequent occurrence:

Cr. J. J. Astor $33, proceeds draft for sale of 40 Muskrat, 4 Bear, 3 Deer, and 12 Mink Skins.

Credit John J. Astor $49.50, proceeds of draft for sale of 400 Skunk Skins.

Cr. John Jacob Astor $131, proceeds of draft on London for £26.10s for sale of 87 Otter Skins, 46 Mink, and 30 Beaver Pelts.

Each year showed a modest increase in the volume of business of the thrifty furrier, but the aggregates were only moderate until the year 1801, being the same year the Canadian trader bought of Mr. Olmsted a portion of Deer Isle, when the volume of bank transactions reached, for the time, enormous dimensions, springing from an aggregate for the year 1799 of $4,011 to over $500,000 for the year 1801. Among the entries in the latter year are two of the same date for checks to Jacques Cartier, the French-Canadian: one for $133.40, drawn "In settlement to date." Inasmuch as in each previous year the aggregate fur transactions with Mr. Cartier had never exceeded $500, an entry of $5,000 seeemed inexplicable on any ordinary grounds.

The enormous growth of Mr. Astor's own transactions also seemed equally mysterious. Mr. Astor had evidently visited England in the year 1801, as the bank entries are filled with credits to him of drafts remitted by him from a Roderick Streeter, varying from £10,000 to £40,000, and aggregating during the year nearly £495,000. Credits of the same Streeter drafts are also made during the two following years to the amount of over $800,000, or a total of over $1,300,000, when the Streeter remittances abruptly cease.

Edwin W. Streeter of London is at the present time one of the largest dealers in precious stones in the world; and as in England the same business is often continued in a family for many generations, it occurred to Mr. Frederick Law Olmsted, who, from the facts already given, had become greatly interested in following the matter to a conclusion, that the Streeter who had made the vast remittances to Mr. Astor might be an ancestor of the present London merchant. An inquiry by mail developed the fact that the present Mr. Streeter is a great-grandson of Roderick Streeter, and that the business had been continued in the family for five generations. Mr. Olmsted sent a confidential agent to London, who succeeded in getting access to the books of the Streeter firm for the years 1798 to 1803, inclusive. Here was found a detailed statement of the transactions with Mr. Astor.

The first item was for £40,000, entered as "Advances on ancient French and Spanish gold coins" deposited by Mr.

Astor, and later another of £4,213.8s for "Balance due for French and Spanish gold coins." All other entries were for the sale of precious stones, mostly diamonds, rubies and pearls which, in all, with the sums paid for the French and Spanish gold, reached the enormous aggregate heretofore given. Certain of the gems were purchased outright by Mr. Streeter, and others were sold by him, as a broker, for the account of Mr. Astor and the proceeds duly remitted during the years 1801–02. The whole account corresponded exactly, item for item, with the various entries of Streeter remittances shown on the books of the Manhattan Bank.

The facts gathered thus far enabled Mr. Olmsted to formulate a theory in substance as follows: That Jacques Cartier had found the box containing the buried treasures of Captain Kidd; that he had taken it to New York and deilvered it to Mr. Astor; that Mr. Astor had bought the contents of the box, or his interest in them, for the check of $5,000; that he had taken the contents to England, and from their sale had realized the vast sums paid him by Mr. Streeter.

Many links in the chain of evidence, however, were still missing, and a great point would be gained if the mysterious box could be traced to the custody of Mr. Astor. It seemed reasonable that this box, if ever in the possession of Mr. Astor, and if its contents were of such great value, would be retained by him with scrupulous care, and that if he had imparted the secret to his children, the box would still be in their possession. If not, it might have been sold as a piece of worthless scrap-iron and lost sight of after the death of the first Mr. Astor. Mr. Olmsted learned that the last house in which the original John Jacob Astor had lived had been torn down in the year 1893, to be replaced by a superb modern building, and that the old building had been sold to a well-known house-wrecking firm for an insignificant sum, as the material was worth but little above the cost of tearing down and removal. In the hope that the rusty box had been sold with other rubbish about the premises, Mr. Olmsted inserted the following advertisement in the New York *Tribune:*

A rusty iron box, strongly made and bolted, was by mistake sold in 1893 to a dealer in junk, supposedly in New York or Brooklyn. The dimensions were 15 x 30 x 15 inches. A person, for sentimental reasons, wishes to reclaim this box, and will pay to its present owner for the same several times its value as scrap-iron. Address F. L., Box 74, New York Tribune.

Within a few days Mr. Olmsted received a letter from Mr. Bronson B. Tuttle of Naugatuck, Connecticut, an iron manufacturer, stating that in a car of scrap-iron bought by him from Melchisedec Jacobs of Brooklyn, was an iron box answering the description given in the *Tribune;* that if it was of any value to the advertiser, it would be forwarded on receipt of eighty cents, which was its cost to him at $11 per ton, the price paid for the carload of scrap.

Mr. Olmsted at once procured the box and shipped it to Deer Isle, where the bolts upon its bottom and the box itself were found to fit perfectly the print in the clay bottom of the cave. The plaster cast of the bottom of the cavity, taken when it was first discovered, matched the bottom of the box as perfectly as ever a casting fitted the mold in which it was made. Every peculiarity in the shape of a bolt-head, every hammer mark made in riveting the bolts, as shown in the clay, was reproduced in the iron box. There was no possible question but that the box was the identical one which had long before been buried in the cave. On the top of the box, too, was distinguishable, despite the heavy coating of rust, in rude and irregularly formed characters, as if made by strokes of a cold-chisel or some similar tool, the letters "W.K."—the initials of the veritable and eminent pirate, Captain William Kidd.

Further inquiry developed the fact that Melchisedec Jacobs, the Brooklyn junk dealer, had purchased the box in a large drayload of scrap-iron, mostly made up of cooking ranges, sashweights, gas, steam and water pipes, etc. from the wrecking firm of Jones & Company; and that Jones & Company had taken such material from the family mansion occupied by the original John Jacob Astor at the time of his death, when tearing it down to make room for the new buildings. The indications thickened that the mysterious box contained the long-lost and widely sought treasures of Captain Kidd. One peculiarity of the box was that there had apparently been no way to open it except by cutting it apart. The top had been firmly riveted in its place, and this fact possibly indicated the reason of its purchase by Mr. Astor at the moderate price of $5,000, since the trader who found it had been unable to open it before his arrival in New York. However, as we have no information on the contract between Mr. Astor and Jacques Cartier, the amount named, $5,000, may have been precisely the percentage agreed upon, which he received upon the profits of his season's business in addition to a salary.

Mr. Olmsted had an accurate copy made of all entries made in the books of the Manhattan Bank as to the transactions of Mr. Astor shown by such books, from 1798 to 1803, and his English agent had similar copies of many letters passing between the parties. The agent also looked up and reported everything available relative to the career of Captain Kidd, the substance of which was as follows:

Captain Kidd had won an enviable reputation in the English and American merchant marine as a brave and intelligent officer. For many years the English merchant vessels had been preyed upon by pirates, numerous vessels were captured and destroyed and others robbed of all their treasure. These depredations were largely along the coast of Madagascar and Mozambique, on the route of the English vessels in the India trade, and off the coasts of South America, where the Spanish galleons bore great treasure from the Peruvian gold fields. The depredations of the pirates became so great that the English merchants finally bought and equipped a stanch war vessel, placed the same under the command of Captain Kidd, and sent him out expressly to chastise and destroy the pirates. As these pirates were known to have secured vast amounts of gold and gems, it was expected that Captain Kidd might not only clear the infested seas of the pirate craft, but capture from them enough treasure to make the operation a profitable one.

After reaching the coast of East Africa, news was received of the destruction by him of sundry piratical vessels containing much treasure, but the capture of this treasure seemed to excite his own cupidity and he decided to engage himself in the occupation of being a malefactor. For some two years thereafter he was literally the scourge of the seas. He plundered alike other pirates and the merchant vessels of every nation. Finally after a cruise along the eastern coast of the United States, as far north as the port of Halifax, he, for some reason, decided boldly to make an entry at the port of Boston as an English merchant vessel, under the papers originally furnished him in England. Before entering Boston Harbor, he put ashore and concealed on Gardiner's Island a considerable quantity of merchandise, consisting largely of bales of valuable silks and velvets, with a small amount of gold and silver and precious stones.

These articles were later discovered and reclaimed by the owners of the vessel, and sold for some £14,000.

From the great number of vessels which he had destroyed and plundered, with their ascertained cargoes, it was known that the treasure thus discovered was but an insignificant fraction of what he had captured—it was known that gold and gems of vast value were somewhere concealed —and thence came the endless searches from Key West and Jekyl Island to Halifax, for the treasure which had thus far seemingly escaped human vision and utterly disappeared. In fact from the little care taken by Captain Kidd as to the plunder hidden on Gardiner's Island, the owners of his ship concluded that to be merely a blind to divert their attention from the vastly greater wealth he had appropriated.

A short time after his arrival in Boston he was arrested and sent to England, and at once put on trial for piracy. In two days he was tried, convicted and hanged. This illustrates the great progress in civilization since that benighted age, for now the most red-handed and popular murderers are allowed months for preparation and trial, are feted, garlanded and made the heroes of the day, and assigned with all priestly assurance to the mansions of the blest. Captain Kidd's wife was not allowed to see him, except for a half hour after the death sentence had been pronounced. They had a whispered conference, and at its close he was seen to hand her a card, upon which he had written the figures, 44106818. This card was taken from her by the guards and never restored, and she even claimed not herself to know. The paper was preserved among the proceedings of the trial, and a photographed copy was secured by Mr. Olmsted.

From the records of the trial, it appeared that Captain Kidd was the only child of his parents; that he had been married for several years; that two children had been born to him, a daughter who died while yet a child and before the trial, and a son who survived both his father and his mother. It also appeared that this son, ten years after his father's execution, enlisted as a private soldier in the English army, and was killed in the battle near Stirling in 1715. The records of the English War Office showed that the widow of this son applied for a pension under the then existing law, and her affidavit and marriage certificate showed her to have been married to the son of Captain Kidd, and that no child had been born to them, and the usual pension was awarded to her and paid until her death in 1744. These facts settled the question as to any claim upon the treasure by descendants of Captain Kidd.

The records of the trial also contained a report by experts upon the card given by Kidd to his wife, to the effect that they had applied to the figures upon it the usual tests for the reading of cipher writings without avail, and that if the figures ever had a meaning, it was undiscoverable. The same conclusion was reached by several people to whom Mr. Olmsted showed the copy of the card. Shortly afterward, when Professor David P. Todd, the astronomer of Amherst College was visiting the family of Mr. Olmsted at Deer Isle, he one day amused himself by calculating the latitude and longitude of the home near the cave, and gave the results to Miss Marion Olmsted. As she was entering these results in her journal, she was struck by the fact that the figures for the latitude, 44° 10′, were the same as the first four figures on the card, 4410, and that the other four figures, 6818, were almost the exact longitude west from Greenwich, which was 68° 17′, a difference easily accounted for by a moderate variation in Captain Kidd's chronometer. The latitude, taken by observation of the pole star, was absolutely accurate. It appeared as though Captain Kidd had told his wife in this manner where to find the hidden treasure, but that, inasmuch as the government authorities had seized the card, she preferred silence toward those who had pursued her husband to his death, and the total loss to everyone of the treasure, rather than, by a confession, to give it into the hands of his enemies. The very simplicity of the supposed cipher writing had been its safeguard, since all the experts had sought for some abstruse and occult meaning in the combination of the figures.

By the happy thought of Miss Olmsted, another link was thus added to the chain of evidence. With the facts given, the only point seemingly needed to show that the Kidd treasure had come into the possession of Mr. Astor was to show that some of the money or gems sold by him had been actually seized by Captain Kidd. Even this, by a happy chance, became possible through the correspondence secured from Mr. Streeter in London.

It appeared that, in the year 1700, Lord and Lady Dunmore were returning to England from India, when the vessel upon which they had taken passage was fired upon and captured by Captain Kidd. His first order was that every person on board should walk the plank into the sea, but several ladies who were passengers pleaded so earnestly for their lives that Kidd finally decided to plunder the cargo and passengers and let the vessel proceed on her voyage. The ladies were compelled, on peril of their lives, to surrender all their jewelry, and among the articles taken from Lady Dunmore was a pair of superb pearl bracelets, the pearls being set in a somewhat peculiar fashion. Another pair, an exact duplicate of those possessed by Lady Dunmore, had been purchased by Lord Dunmore as a wedding present to his sister, and the story of the two pairs of pearls, which were of great value, and of her pleading for her life to Captain Kidd, is a matter of history, as well as one of the cherished family traditions.

In 1801, Roderick Streeter wrote to Mr. Astor that the then Lady Dunmore, in looking over some gems which he was offering her, had seen a pair of exquisite pearl bracelets which were a part of the Astor consignment, and had at once recognized them as the identical pair taken by Kidd nearly one hundred years before. She returned the following day with the family solicitor, bringing the duplicate bracelets; told and verified the story of the loss of one pair by Lady Dunmore; compaired the two pairs, showing their almost perfect identity, showing certain private marks upon each and demonstrating beyond question that the pearls offered by Mr. Streeter were the identical gems seized by Captain Kidd. The solicitor demanded their surrender to Lady Dunmore on the ground that, having been stolen, no property rights in them could pass even to an innocent purchaser.

Mr. Streeter then stated that he had asked for delay until he could communicate with the owner of the gems, and had asked Mr. Astor for instructions. Mr. Astor replied, authorizing the delivery of the bracelets to Lady Dunmore, and asking Mr. Streeter to assure her that the supposed owner was guiltless of wrong in the matter and was an entirely innocent holder. He repeated the caution, given also in sundry other letters, that to no one was the ownership of the gems sold by Mr. Streeter to be revealed. They were to be sold as the property of Streeter, acquired in the regular course of business. Lady Dunmore afterward sat to Sir Thomas Lawrence for her portrait, and was painted wearing upon her arms the pearl bracelets thus curiously reclaimed. This portrait is considered one of the masterpieces of Lawrence.

By the discovery of the hole in a cave in Maine, after a lapse of two hundred years, was thus curiously brought to light the apparent origin of the colossal Astor fortune.

Prior to the acquisition of the Kidd treasures by the first American Astor, he was simply a modest trader, earning each year, by frugality and thrift, two or three hundred dollars above his living expenses, with a fair prospect of accumulating, by an industrious life, a fortune of twenty or thirty thousand dollars. When he became possessed of the Kidd plunder, he handled it with the skill of a great general. He expanded his fur trade until it embraced the continent. The record of his checks given during the three years when he received the $1,300,000 shows that he expanded over $700,000 of the amount in the purchase of real estate in the City of New York. The entries of the various checks are recorded as "Payment for the Wall Street property," the "Bond Street land," then "Broadway Corner," etc., the descriptions being sufficiently accurate, when verified by comparison with the titles of record, to locate at this date every parcel of land bought, all of which is still in the possession of the Astor family. Some twenty different tracts of land in what is now the very heart of the business and residence portion of New York were thus purchased, each one of which is now probably of more value than the price originally paid for the whole.

In obtaining a knowledge of the various details already given, over two years had been spent by Mr. Olmsted and his agents. The results seemingly reached may be summarized as follows:

1. Captain Kidd had sailed along the Maine coast shortly before his arrest, and an iron box marked with his initials was afterward taken from the cave into Mr. Astor's possession.

2. Jacques Cartier had camped for many years, while employed by Mr. Astor, immediately adjoining the cave where the box was concealed, and his rapid increase in wealth and that of Mr. Astor were simultaneous.

3. Mr. Astor's great wealth came from the sale, through Mr. Streeter, of ancient Spanish and French gold, and of gems, some of which were proved to have been a part of the spoils of Captain Kidd, which made it a reasonable presumption that all of such property was of the same character.

4. Captain Kidd was known to have captured and somewhere concealed gold and gems of vast value, and the card given his wife before his execution indicated, by a plausible reading, the cave upon Mr. Olmsted's land as the place of concealment.

5. The family of Captain Kidd had long been extinct, and no one could successfully contest with Mr. Olmsted the ownership of the property concealed upon his land.

Having his evidence thus formulated, Mr. Olmsted called upon the descendants of Mr. Astor, accompanied by his attorney, Mr. William M. Evarts, and demanded of them: 1. A payment by them to him of the sum of $1,300,-000, the amount received of Mr. Streeter, with interest from the date of its receipt. The total amount, computed according to the laws of New York in force since 1796, was $5,112,234.80; and Mr. Olmsted offered, on condition of immediate cash payment, to deduct the item of $34.80. This demand was refused. 2. Mr. Olmsted then demanded that the Astor family should convey to him all the real estate in New York City purchased by their ancestor with the money received from Mr. Streeter, with the accrued rents and profits from the date of its purchase, and this demand was likewise refused.

These refusals left to Mr. Olmsted no alternative except to resort to the courts for the establishment of his rights, and an action was accordingly commenced. The declaration filed by his attorneys, Joseph H. Choate, Steward L. Woodford and Frederick W. Holls, set out in full the history of the claim from the beginning, as has been detailed herein, and petitions the court for alternative relief; either that the descendants of John Jacob Astor pay to Mr. Olmsted the sum of $1,300,000 with interest from the time of its receipt by Mr. Astor; or, failing in this, that Mr. Astor be adjudged a trustee for the rightful owner of the money thus received, and that the property purchased with such funds be ordered conveyed to Mr. Olmsted.

To this declaration the Astor family, by their solicitors, Elihu Root and Edward S. Isham, answered, denying all liability, upon the ground that the cause of action, if ever valid, was barred by the statute of limitations. To this answer the plaintiffs demurred, alleging for grounds thereof that it appeared clearly from the pleadings that Mr. Olmsted had been vigilant in the assertion of his claim as soon as reasonable proof of its existence came to his knowledge, and further, that the statute of limitations did not run as against a trust. The demurrer was sustained by the court upon both grounds, the court intimating, however, that when the case came to a hearing the plaintiff must select and rest his case on one or the other form of relief demanded, and could not, in the same action, secure the alternative relief sought. After this decision the defendants filed a general denial of all the claims of Mr. Olmsted.

This is the present status of litigation, and it is expected that the case will be brought to a final trial during the present year.

Should the judgment upon the trial be in favor of Mr. Olmsted, or even against him upon some technical ground, it would, in either event, be a great boon to the people along our Atlantic seaboard, in that it will reveal the actual fate of the Kidd treasures. The publicity upon this point will stop the ceaseless and fruitless expenditure of money in digging for such hidden wealth, as well as the exactions of clairvoyants, Indian spiritual mediums, rappers, professional ghosts and witch-hazel experts, who have yearly preyed on the credulity of their victims in locating the Kidd deposits.

From the dramatic character of the claim, from the eminent ability of the counsel for each contestant and from the large amount involved, it is needless to add that the trial will be watched with intense interest, and that it will stand as the cause célèbre of our century.

COMMENTARY UPON "A NOTABLE LAWSUIT"
BY FREDERICK L. OLMSTED

This interesting and amusing yarn has been in private circulation and has appeared from time to time in the newspapers in garbled form since 1894. In that year it was written for the amusement of the author, Mr. Franklin H. Head, and Miss Olmsted, and was subsequently read before a small literary club in Chicago of which the author was a member. Intended as a burlesque hoax, it was so written as to carry a pervading atmosphere of serious verisimilitude, interwoven with enough of the preposterous to let the reader gradually catch on to the joke. It is a delightful example of this type of yarn.

Unfortunately, in passing from hand to hand, and especially from mouth to mouth, it has often lost its delightful humorous quality and becomes a bald hoax story, arousing various degrees either of credulity or of speculation as to what possible basis in fact was a dinner conversation between the author and Miss Olmsted, in Chicago, during which they talked about legends of Captain Kidd, about Penobscot Bay and the land which her father had then recently purchased there, and about a sort of hollow in the rocks on the shore of that land almost big enough to call a cave and almost fit to weave some kind of romantic legend about. Miss Olmsted may even have said that a chest of buried treasure would be indispensable for the proper sort of legend, and may have indicated her willingness to stretch the size of the cave as much as might be necessary to make room for a chest of suitable dimensions.

The seed was planted, and in the fertile soil of the author's imagination soon produced the full-grown story, bristling with apparent facts. It is hardly surpassed by his pseudoscientific monograph, in the manner of the higher criticism, 'Shakespeare's Insomnia.'

It has been pleasing and amusing to explain all this to my many friends, but it is getting to be something of a bore to explain it individually to unnumbered eager inquirers.

FREDERICK LAW OLMSTED

In March of 1950 I talked with Miss Carolyn Olmsted, who, with her sister, owns the "Binnical" cottage on that part of Deer Isle located to the southwest of Small's Cove. It was believed that the original cave was under the porch of the old Felsted home, which first was a private house. Miss Olmsted assured me that this belief was incorrect, and gave me particulars about the actual cave which Mr. Franklin H. Head chose as the scene of his fictitious story about Captain Kidd and the Astor fortune.

"The cave is all solid rock, of course," Miss Olmsted began, "and when the tide is half in, the bow of your boat can be inserted into the mouth of the cave. At low tide the cave is about five feet high, and nine or ten feet wide. I have stood inside the cave with two others and there was room for all three of us and a little bit more. Our cottage is quite a distance from the cave, about a mile or more through the woods and there is no residence or building near the cave and never has been in my memory. Incidentally, Mr. Head never intended that his story should be published, as it was just for the reading pleasure of Mr. Head, Miss Marion Olmsted and a small literary club."

In June 1950 I visited the cave and found it essentially as described by Miss Carolyn Olmsted.

XXIV

Oak Island, 1972

Last October Mrs. Snow and I were guests of David Tobias at dinner in Montreal. The genius behind the remarkable activity now going on at Oak Island's Money Pit, Mr. Tobias is the deepest thinker of all the scores of persons anxious to find the answer to that tantalizing mystery.

It is now half a century since my first written comments on Oak Island in Nova Scotia were published. For one brief period in his existence, Oak Island's legendary Frederick Blair lived less than two hundred yards from my house in Winthrop, Massachusetts, and quite often he would rightfully object to our coasting down Hillside Avenue and sliding up on his sidewalk. I never knew then that he was a dedicated treasure seeker and had invested tens of thousands of dollars in a plan to obtain the fabulous Oak Island treasure.

When he moved to Brookline he set up an office in Boston and obtained financial help to buy machinery and supplies for what he believed would yield him about ten million dollars. Later, I flew to Amherst, Nova Scotia, where he was Registrar of Deeds in the court there. He still had his enthusiasm for solving the enigma of Oak Island, but his money for such ventures had all been expended.

During the long period of our association with each other, we exchanged many letters. Blair kept up his enthusiasm until the last. In 1950 he called me long distance from Amherst and told me that the doctors had informed him that he was not long for this world.

"Mr. Snow, we get the Bruins hockey on our radios here and I am a fan of them. Still, I will never forget Boston's association with my early years, and my thoughts go back to you and your visits to Oak Island more than you probably realize. I would die happy tonight if the question which I give you could be answered before I pass on. That question is 'Who buried what at Oak Island?' "

I believe I have received more letters about Oak Island than on any other subject. I have saved over one thousand communications sent to me from every continent, and I am still impressed by man's insatiable desire to answer the question Frederick Blair put to me the last time I ever heard his voice.

Indeed, the treasure site at Oak Island, thirty miles south of Halifax, has mystified and fascinated millions of persons since 1795. Several months ago I visited the backers of a new company which even now is sending down into the bowels of the earth new machines designed solely to solve for all time this weird mystery. Since 1795 no fewer than thirty-seven shafts and pits of almost every shape and size have been sunk at the eastern side of the island. The present group of treasure hunters, Triton Alliance, is a syndicate of prominent Canadian businessmen who have set aside the largest sum yet, $460,000, to find out what lies beneath the surface of Oak Island. As a result, they may succeed where others failed. Almost every past attempt has ended when funds ran out. The decision of the Alliance to go ahead followed the drilling of no fewer than fifty test holes.

Oak Island lies in Mahone Bay. Approximately two and a half miles long and a mile wide, the island is an ideal location for buried treasure. It is protected from the ocean by the bay and until recently was far enough offshore to be completely secluded. A causeway now connects the mainland with the island.

Sometime in the eighteenth century, and perhaps earlier, a group of people dug a pit about twelve feet in diameter and more than one hundred feet deep. The pit was connected underground with the ocean, 460 feet away. At the bottom of the pit were placed large wooden containers of metal or coins. It is assumed that the metal or coins must have been of considerable number and value because of the extensive efforts to conceal the treasure.

First indications of the existence of the treasure were found in the fall of 1795 by three boys from Chester on the mainland—Daniel McInnis, Anthony Vaughn, and Jack Smith, who had gone hunting on the then deserted island. About four hundred feet in from shore they came upon a tall oak tree with a branch sawed off in such a way as to appear that a heavy hoist or cable had been used there. Examining the ground, the boys noticed a slight depression, about twelve feet in diameter, directly under the sawed-off limb. They studied the land nearby but found no other clues and returned home.

Early the next day they returned with picks and shovels. As they began to dig, they noticed that the earth was softer within the twelve-foot circle than outside, confirming their belief that the ground had been previously shoveled. They also detected strange, picklike scratches at the outside rim of the circle as they dug deeper.

At a depth of ten feet, they hit a wooden plank which they were confident was protection for a treasure chest. But the obstruction was merely a platform of logs. When they removed it, they found nothing but earth below. Discouraged and weary, they paddled back to the mainland.

But sleep soothes tired backs and weary bodies, and at the next opportunity they again went out to the island. When they had dug twenty feet down, they struck another platform. But again there was nothing but earth under the logs.

Week after week, month after month, the boys went out to the island whenever they could. Eventually, the project became too much for them; they needed special equipment and engineers to advise them. While they were planning to arrange for help, snowstorms forced them to discontinue their efforts for the winter.

Back in Chester, the three boys began talking about their activities. An old woman with whom they conversed revealed a strange story her grandmother had related years before. In 1720 the people of the mainland had observed strange lights burning on Oak Island at night. Boatmen curious enough to cruise in the vicinity had seen outlines of men believed to be pirates silhouetted against giant bonfires. Two fishermen who went to Oak Island to investigate never returned. Finally the pirates, if such they were, disappeared from Mahone Bay, and the area settled down again. But the women of Chester, whose men had vanished, never forgot the pirates.

A feeling of terror toward the island persisted from the 1720s, and the three boys found it impossible to get a sponsor for their project. The years passed and no further attempts were made to locate the treasure, if treasure there was. The boys grew to manhood and married. Dan Mc-Innis and Jack Smith settled on Oak Island itself, but Anthony Vaughn moved to a house on the mainland.

Later, according to legend, Jack Smith's wife did not want their first baby to be born on Oak Island because of its mysterious history. The couple traveled to Truro, Nova Scotia, and stayed at the home of a Dr. John Lynds. When the mother and baby returned to Oak Island, Dr. Lynds came along with them. He had been bitten by the treasure bug and wished to see the island for himself. When the doctor was offered payment for his services, he is said to have refused and suggested that his fee should consist of one share of a treasure-seeking company. In this strange manner the first Oak Island treasure company came into being.

Dr. Lynds made an exhaustive study of the scene where the pit had been dug. Examining the tree, he found marks and figures on its trunk, and noticed that the branch which had been sawed off was the largest of all the branches, and had projected directly over the center of the pit itself.

Inspecting the planking, Dr. Lynds found that the ends of the logs had been imbedded in the sides of the pit to prevent the earth from settling at the surface—a depression which eventually might lead to the hiding place.

Dr. Lynds climbed into the pit and scraped at the final tier of logs, thirty feet below the surface, where the boys had ceased their labors. Later he examined a strange ringbolt attached to one of the beach boulders.

The doctor then traveled to Halifax and persuaded several prominent men to join in forming the nucleus of a treasure company. Before long, equipment began arriving on the island.

Deeper and deeper the diggers went. At forty feet, fifty

feet, and sixty feet platforms were reached and passed. At seventy and eighty feet the platforms contained strange fiberlike material placed next to charcoal. A substance resembling putty was found at another level.

At ninety feet the greatest mystery of all awaited the diggers. It was a flat stone, about three feet across and sixteen inches wide. On the face of the stone curious characters had been cut. The Reverend A. T. Kempton of Cambridge, Massachusetts, said in 1940 that the characters indicated that "Forty feet below two million pounds are buried."

One Saturday evening shortly after the stone had been found, the men reached a depth of ninety-five feet. An iron bar was shoved down through the bottom of the pit and three feet deeper a wooden platform was struck. The men then stopped work for the weekend. When they returned Monday morning, water had filled the shaft to within thirty-five feet of the surface.

The men worked day and night in an effort to bail it out, but the water remained at the same level.

Finally, in desperation, they sank another nearby shaft to drain the pit. In a short time the new shaft reached 110 feet, and then a tunnel was driven horizontally across to the money pit. Suddenly water burst in and flooded both shafts and the tunnel as well. The discouraged treasure hunters, their funds exhausted, abandoned their activities and returned to the mainland.

The continuous flooding of the treasure shaft may have been caused by the removal of the strange flat stone. Perhaps it had been placed there to defeat anyone who persevered to the depth of ninety feet underground.

The years went by and grass covered the entrance to both pits at Oak Island. Not until the California Gold Rush of 1849 was enough enthusiasm kindled to float another organization. Dr. Lynds and Anthony Vaughn of the original company were still alive and gave the manager of the new project much valuable information. Both expressed their confidence that the treasure was still at the bottom of the money pit.

Digging began soon afterward, and the eighty-six-foot mark was attained before water again came pouring in. Bailing casks were sent down, but no further progress could be made.

Primitive boring apparatus of the type used by coal miners was taken out to the island and placed in charge of J. B. McCully of Truro. He ordered a platform built about thirty feet down in the money pit, just above the reach of the water. The boring began with a pod auger.

A platform was struck at ninety-six feet. The auger went through the platform, which was five inches thick, dropped through space for twelve inches, then went through four inches of wood. A little farther down the auger struck loose metal.

Unfortunately, none of the metal pieces could be brought up. The auger then traveled through eight more inches of wood, then twenty-two inches of metal, four inches of wood, and six more inches of wood, after which it hit clay.

John Gamel, a stockholder, late one day watched foreman John Pitblado remove something from the auger, wash it, and slide it into his pocket. When questioned by Gamel, Pitblado said that it would be revealed at the next stockholders' meeting. That night he vanished from the island. He was killed the following month in a gold mining accident.

The years went by. Now and then a discovery would be made, such as a coin said to have the date 1713, but none was authenticated.

It was in August 1892 that Frederick Leander Blair opened his unusual office at 4 Liberty Square in Boston for the express purpose of raising money to bring up the Oak Island treasure. From 1892 until his death on April 1, 1951, Blair devoted his life to trying to find the treasure. He failed.

The present company, Triton Alliance, arranged for drilling with Becker Drills, Ltd., of Toronto and Warnock Hersey International, Ltd., of Montreal. The two firms concentrated in an area where two old shafts had been sunk, very near to where it is believed the original money pit was located. Bedrock here is between 160 and 170 feet down.

All concerned now agree that it is impossible any previous searcher ever sank a shaft this deep. Therefore, it was without question vital when the drilling revealed a clearly defined depression in the bedrock approximately fifty feet deep and thirty feet across almost directly below a relatively recent exploration, that of Gilbert D. Hedden in 1934.

This depression was filled with heavy putty-like blue clay in which layers of small stones were found regularly every eighteen inches or so. In the opinion of a leading mining expert, Major-General Colin Campbell, this indicates that human thought planned and carried out the distribution of small stones.

Several tiny oak buds were found embedded in the clay ten feet or so below the bedrock surface, and a small piece of brass was found, evidently wrenched from a larger body. Right now this fragment of brass is being carefully studied at McGill by metallurgists, whose first finding is that the brass definitely was smelted before the year 1850; how much before has not been determined.

Carbon 14 tests of the wood chips brought up from

cavity areas indicate their growth period as definitely between 1490 and 1660. The area where the chips were found was about thirty feet below bedrock. The drill, on two occasions, went through forty feet of bedrock, then wood, then a thin layer of the blue clay, and finally the cavity, before again hitting bedrock. This indicated the presence of human-placed cribbing.

A famous underground water expert, Dr. Hugh Golder, is also conducting tests on the island. Dr. Golder is drilling a series of bore-holes to decide on the porosity of the soil and the water pressure. He is also conducting dye tests to find out all he can about where the water is coming from and whether it could be intercepted. In tight areas a special television camera two and a half inches in size will be lowered to provide visual information.

When Mrs. Snow and I were guests of David Tobias in Montreal, he seemed confident that the mystery would be solved once and for all, but I cannot forget the comment of Frederick Blair's uncle, who wrote in 1896:

"I saw enough to convince me that there was treasure buried there and enough to convince me that they will never get it."

XXV

Searching for Gold

My interest in gold, sunken treasure, and pirates began
in a strange way when I was four years of age. My older
brother Nicholas, then twelve, was showing a group of his
chums Grandfather's collection of foreign curios. All of
the boys gathered in our parlor. They were looking high
on the wall where hung a pirate's poison dagger. Grandfather Joshua Rowe had captured the dagger after killing
the pirate who had held it in a personal duel fought between them, now more than a century ago. At the time of
the encounter Grandfather was one of the crew aboard
the wrecked clipper ship *Crystal Palace,* which was ashore
on the island of Mindanao, near Zamboanga.

Nicholas was explaining with particular emphasis that
the weapon on the wall was a real pirate's dagger. He
jumped up on a chair and pulled the ancient relic down.
Withdrawing the dagger from its scabbard, he held it high.

"If I cut you, you'll die a horrible death from this native
poison!"

Just then Mother heard the commotion as Nicholas

chased the other boys around the parlor. Running to the door, she almost fainted when she saw what was happening.

"Nicholas, for heaven's sake, put that dagger down. Let me have it."

"No, Mother, I'll put it away myself," said the boy. But in the confusion Mother received a gash in her hand.

"Oh, I am cut! What shall I do? The poison will kill me," cried Mother. It was a terrible situation, and I will always remember her solemn warning. Mother did not die; in fact, the cut had not penetrated beyond the outer skin. However, the next day Mother took us all in the parlor and made us promise never again to touch the poison dagger. She told us in such a dramatic manner and with such vivid imagery that we never forgot her words of caution.

Before I was twelve, thanks to the help of my older brother Win and our father, I could swim on and below the water, and soon was diving under the schooners that came into old Lewis Wharf near the Merriman Fish Market in Winthrop. Great loads of cut stones would come in from Maine. At high tide I would dive from the wharf, swim under the keel of the schooner, and come up on the other side. I never dared to do it at low tide because quite often the keel was deeply imbedded in the mud.

As the years went by I became more and more interested in the bottom of the sea.* I recall a Boston newspaper planning and putting on a moving picture of land and sea and using the Winthrop Beach area for filming some of the scenes. In one of the episodes a car was pushed off the cliff where the Winthrop water tower stands today. The star of

* The New England Scuba Diving Fraternity have accepted me as one of the few scuba divers who date back their early diving activities to before World War I. Of course, the technical scuba diver did not come into being until much later, but I brought up my first real treasure from the sea before World War I.

the moving picture, who was supposed to be struggling for her life offshore from the cliff, lost one of her sneakers in fairly deep water that afternoon, and I dove far down and brought it up, making me the local hero for several weeks.

Then when we moved to Marshfield in 1950 I began exploring under water off the Fourth Cliff near our house. Spurred on by the knowledge that a load of grindstones from a shipwreck was in water nearby, a group of us, including Jerry Thomas, attempted to find the stones, but all we did was to attract a colony of sharks swimming in pairs. We gave up.

Four years later Donald Hourihan did find one of the grindstones, several of which had been brought to the surface from the 1830 wreck by Alfred Damon in 1876.

I explored down toward Brant Rock in Marshfield. In particular I was anxious to find the bones of the French galleon that sank in the great storm of 1616. Only one man was saved, and his name is believed to be Peter Wallis. Captured shortly after the wreck by Indians, Wallis was taken to what is now Middleboro, then called Nummastaquyt, where he remained as a captive for three years.

Then on May 19, 1619, Captain Thomas Dermer set sail from Monhegan Island in "an open Pinnace" and "passed along the coast" to arrive in Plymouth. Finding most of the Indians dead from a plague, Dermer "travelled alongst a daies journey Westward" until he reached Middleboro, where "I redeemed a Frenchman."

Peter Wallis, the redeemed Frenchman, was allowed to settle in what is now Pembroke, where his orchard and his well can be seen off Route 14 to this day!

Back at Marshfield the great galleon slowly went to pieces at the bottom of the sea, and it was not until around 1880 that a chance dive brought the old wreck to light. At that time a friend of the late Adelaide Hildreth Burgess of

Brant Rock owned an expensive shotgun. He lost it one day while out on Brant Rock hunting ducks and summoned a diver down from Boston. The diver never found the shotgun but among other things he brought up were two blunderbusses and a cannon from the ancient galleon. Later, cannon balls and grape shot were found in the area, the last grape shot being discovered by Parker Phillips of Brant Rock several years ago.

Mrs. Burgess told me shortly before her death that a fragment of the old wreck was reputedly buried close to the Brant Rock ledge itself. The keel of the galleon was discovered after a storm in 1953 had scrubbed out the sand from the area, and occasional diving operations have been going on from time to time ever since.

Diver John Light has made the most important find.* At dead-low tide on December 6, 1953, he went overboard at the scene of the wreck, where a buoy had been connected to a grapnel on the bottom. His statement follows:

"On December 6 I descended to the bottom in thirty-five feet of water off Brant Rock. I found the grapnel, which was stuck between two rocks. I freed it, came back about ten or fifteen feet and found myself on something which was hard, smooth and even. It seemed like metal or rock. I went down eight inches with my right foot. I was facing west, in the general direction of the boat.

"I got my other foot off the object, but the visibility was only six inches. The water was extremely roiled because of the recent storm. I knelt down beside the object, turned around, and faced back. Then I examined it and found that I could push my arms way inside under the object.

"I found that the object was of metal, man-made, about two inches thick all the way. It was about nine feet from one end to the other, and six feet across. It came out of the

---

* Later he made scores of dives to the famed *Lusitania* off Ireland.

mud at a slant. The object appeared to be a great slab of iron. It wasn't jagged but smooth and could very well have been the caboose of a galleon.

"After I examined it I ran into the fluke of what was a very large anchor. It was probably about ten feet long, possibly fifteen feet. It was about fourteen inches out of the sand, and apparently came out of the sand at a slight angle, indicating that the other fluke, from the size of the one showing, was directly below, about eight feet distant. The fluke was from four to five inches thick."

That December day, I interviewed fisherman Charles Newton of Island Street, Brant Rock, who told of two more anchors, one in Brant Rock Cove and the other in the area right off Blue Stone at Ocean Bluffs. One of the anchors was very large and heavy and had a wooden crosspiece. Newton and his brother Bob had hooked on to the anchor and dragged it in about one hundred yards when the line parted and they had to leave it there. The other anchor, relatively close to a location off the Mullen residence, had the fluke and part of the arm showing out of the mud in about twenty-five feet of water at half tide.

When John Light found the fragment, he set the grapple underneath and buoyed the location. All the following winter of 1953–54 Jim Mullen, who was flying in a plane over the region, noticed the buoy bobbing up and down in the water. Unfortunately a March northeaster swept in across Brant Rock and the buoy was snapped off. Repeated attempts to relocate the fragment have failed, possibly because sand has now covered the location to a depth of from four to seven feet, according to the estimates of lobstermen who fish in the vicinity. Several thousand dollars' worth of pieces of eight may still be at the bottom there.

In 1953 an old shield, fragments of a conquistador's helmet, a small anchor, and more than a score of pieces of eight were recovered and brought to the surface. Metallurgists have indicated that the anchor brought up off Brant Rock and the ancient shield also taken from the same area are of the period between 1575 and 1630. They were both heavily caked with sea cement, hard-caked sand and stones possibly created by chemical reaction as the salt water reacts on the metal.

On Wednesday, August 24, 1955, it was reported that C. Thomas Burgess, Jr., a fourteen-year-old skin diver whose summer house was fairly close to the area, went down to the bottom and recovered a heavy water-soaked fragment of the ancient vessel. Later I presented that same fragment of the 1616 shipwreck to Curator Warren Strong at the Pilgrim Museum at Plymouth, where it is today.

In order to recover additional relics or curios from the wreck more work is necessary, and success depends on the storms that sweep in across New England in the winter months.

Down in Florida, however, business is booming in the Spanish galleon field, and it is mostly because of Kip Wagner.

This treasure seeker, whose talents are being noted up and down the Atlantic Coast, retired from house-building in 1955 to continue searching the sands of Florida, onshore and off the beaches. In that year a hurricane had just swept the shores, and Kip found a cob piece of eight, his fortieth find.

Studying the Bernard Romans chart of 1774, he located the part of Florida which showed the spot where the galleon victims of the 1715 gale had gone ashore.

Eventually he located a cannon, which decided him on starting a company known today as the Real Eight Company. The group made arrangements with the State of

Florida whereby they would be permitted to keep 75 per
cent of what they found on the sea bottom and the State
would get the remainder.

They found a mass of silver coins weighing about fifty
pounds and by electrolytic reduction they salvaged many
of the coins. Business continued favorable, and by 1966
there was so much treasure in the company's possession
that the group held its first public auction. They realized
$472,020 from the sale. It was indeed a remarkable auction,
showing that terrific progress in treasure hunting has been
made.

Probably fifty million dollars is still to be found in the
area. In 1944 I wrote in my *Pirates and Buccaneers* that
$35,000,000 lies buried in the Atlantic, with five per cent
of this to be recovered in the foreseeable future, a statement at which everyone scoffed. With the aid of two-way
radios, dredges, drills large enough to contain men as they
bore into the bottom, air lifts, and unbelievably sensitive
magnetometers, my prediction already is more than coming true.

The air lift has been replaced by the prop wash, which
actually was invented by oystermen anxious to clear away
the mud from their oyster beds. The prop wash is a six-
foot aluminum pipe, two feet in diameter, which can be
fitted to a craft's transom.

Aiming the craft's propeller downward, the pipe op-
erates over a single area after the craft is anchored bow and
stern. It can do in fifteen minutes the amount of scouring
for which a diver with an air lift would need nine hours
and a half.

The effectiveness of the prop wash extends to no less
than forty feet down from the surface of the sea. There are
enough galleons awaiting divers to that depth to keep the
scuba fraternity busy for the rest of the present century.

XXVI

Gold in the Sea

Millions in treasure are buried in the seven seas of this world, most of which will never be brought to the surface. This chapter tells of countless riches that have been salvaged from the ocean. In each individual case these have amounted to infinitely more than a king's ransom. Author Frank H. Shaw stated it best in 1930 when he said, "The sea plays with loaded dice." When a roll of the dice means a million dollars, then indeed Shaw told the truth.

The loss of four craft, the *General Grant* in 1866, the *Laurentic* in 1917, the *Egypt* in 1923, and the *Niagara* in 1940, seem to emphasize Shaw's statement. If we can accept the most conservative estimates concerning the amount of gold lost on these four vessels, it would amount to more than fifty million dollars.

I believe that the loss of the *General Grant* impressed me more than any of the three others, probably because of the truly improbable wrecking of a large clipper ship inside a gigantic cave.

When the *General Grant* sank to her doom at Disappointment Island, Tuamotu, near Auckland, she carried an estimated six to nine million dollars in gold, wool, zinc ore, and general cargo. The details follow.

The clipper *General Grant,* under command of Captain William Loughlin, sailed out of Port Philip Bay for London on May 4, 1866. In addition to her valuable cargo, she carried more than one hundred passengers.

Two days out of Port Philip, the ship encountered a storm and was driven off course by the heavy seas and winds. Captain Loughlin tried to maintain a straight course between Disappointment Island and the main island of the Auckland group, but the force of the storm carried the vessel head-on toward the cliffs.

On May 13, 1866, the *General Grant* struck the rocks. Her mainmast snapped and broke clean off. The craft, her masts and spars crunching and falling all around, battered her way through an opening that led into the great abysmal darkness. She wedged herself against the cliffs of a cave. In the complete blackness of the vast cavern, the seamen hung lanterns to the ship's taffrail, and soon the flickering light illuminated the rocky vault in which the men found themselves. They could now see that the craft was battered beyond all hope.

The next morning the sailors lowered the small boats, hoping to row out of the cave in safety. But in their rush to enter the boats, the passengers panicked and scores were lost overboard. An hour later only thirteen of the ship's company were still alive. As the thirteen rowed outside the cavern's entrance, they looked back to see Captain Loughlin waving his handkerchief in farewell from the deck of the foundering vessel. A short time later, with a terrible hissing sound, the *General Grant* sank beneath the waves.

Making for the nearest shore, the men beached their

craft and pulled the lifeboat above the reach of the sea. They collected a tremendous amount of driftwood and started a bonfire which they kept burning constantly day after day, hoping that the blaze would attract some passing ship. But few were the ships that ever took a route passing close enough to Disappointment Island. Lloyd's, in London, declared the *General Grant* missing at sea.

On the island, the men lived on goats, pigs, and seals. A crewman of the *Grant* carved a message on a small ship model, which was put in the sea and soon vanished from sight. Months later it was picked up by the whaler *Amherst*. The ship went to the rescue of the handful of survivors, reaching them in December 1867. On the way back to civilization, the survivors explained how for eighteen months they had watched for passing sails in vain.

In 1885 an Australian syndicate made a futile attempt to locate the gold cargo in the cave. Then year after year other groups tried to salvage the treasure. Finally, New Zealand claimed the wreck and began leasing salvage rights. In 1968 it was reported that more than three million dollars had been found, but confirmation is lacking.

At the height of World War I, in January 1917, the White Star liner *Laurentic* was sunk by a mine off the mouth of Lough Swilly, near the Irish Sea, in twenty-two fathoms. More than 350 people drowned. Extremely important to the Allied cause at the time was the hoped-for recovery of $20,000,000 in gold aboard the liner. The gold could be exchanged for desperately needed wartime goods from America.

Even though it was midwinter, the British government ordered an all-out effort to recover the 3210 bars of gold aboard the *Laurentic*. Captain G. C. C. Damant, a diving expert, took over the task and soon was making good progress. Diver E. C. Miller discovered that the *Laurentic* had taken a sixty-degree list to rest on her port side. Miller located the starboard entry port, blew it open with gun cotton, reached the bullion room and found the gold.

Each box was about ten inches square and six inches deep, weighed 137 pounds, and was worth $30,000. Struggling with superhuman effort along the slanted deck, by noon the next day Miller had four boxes safely aboard the salvage craft. Unfortunately the rest of the treasure slid down and out of the strong room before Miller could reach it again, for a violent northerly gale pounded the area for a full week.

Miller now had to devise a new entry method, for he realized that the storm had dropped the gold down into the port bilge. After shoring up the vital area where they were working, the divers continued their dangerous salvage attempts. Diver Blackford on one occasion was trapped under a steel plate. Diver Clear went down and took charge of the rescue, which was carried out successfully.

By September $3,000,000 of the gold had been brought up, but when the United States entered the war, the urgency was at an end.

The recovery of the treasure continued. In 1920 and 1921 only fifty bars were brought up, but in 1922 no less than six million dollars in gold came to the surface. Probably the largest amount of gold ever brought up from a wreck in a single year was in 1923, when eight million dollars in gold was raised to the surface and stacked aboard the recovery craft.

A total of ninety-nine per cent of the *Laurentic*'s gold, valued at twenty million dollars, had been brought up.

In 1922 another craft was reported in Lloyd's List as having gone down. She was the P. & O. liner *Egypt,* which on May 22, 1922, collided with the French steamer *Seine*. She sank off Ushant, Brittany, taking with her eighty-eight men and $10,000,000 in gold and silver.

Peter Sandberg of Sweden, Alain Terme of France, and Commendatore Quaglia of Genoa united to form a group to bring up the *Egypt*'s gold. Quaglia had a superb salvage craft, the *Artiglio*.

Salvage progress on the *Egypt* was painfully slow between 1922 and 1929, with nothing of importance accomplished. Finally December 7, 1930, arrived. This was the day when the *Artiglio* was to detonate a substantial amount of explosives to clear the approaches to the island of Hovet of an American craft that was on the bottom. The explosion, however, overwhelmed the watchers, the gigantic wave killing twelve out of nineteen aboard the *Artiglio*, which was destroyed.

Not to be denied, Quaglia built another salvage craft, the *Artiglio II*. The new vessel steadfastly worked on the problem of bringing up gold from the *Egypt*, and on June 22, 1932, the drag came to the surface, deposited its load on deck, and two shiny yellow bars of gold dropped out. On June 25, 1932, £80,000 of gold were taken to Plymouth, England, for inspection by Lloyds. The years of effort had paid off!

By November 7 a total of 865 gold bars was recovered. Up from the bottom were £83,300 in gold and £11,023 pounds of silver. By the end of the following year almost everything of value had been removed from the *Egypt* where she lay on the bottom of the sea.

At three thirty-four in the morning of July 19, 1940, the liner *Niagara* was blown up by a mine. She had left Auckland a short time before, loaded with ten million dollars in gold, and encountered the mine thirty miles out to sea from Whangarei Harbor, New Zealand. It was later decided that the Nazi raider *Orion* probably had placed the device.

The newly equipped *Daymore* was ordered to attempt locating the *Niagara* and bring up her vitally needed gold from the almost impossible depth of 438 feet.

A diving bell or observation turret was constructed and brought to the area where it was believed the *Niagara* went down. Diver J. E. Johnstone, an outstanding underwater explorer of the region, was engaged for the dangerous task ahead.

Johnno, as he was called, went to the bottom with the bell in four hundred feet of water and positively identified the *Niagara*, which was lying on her side with a list of seventy degrees.

A journalist on the Sydney *Morning Herald* in Australia, James Taylor, wrote a book about Johnstone, and tells of the first visit to the *Niagara* in the diving bell.

Johnno descended to the *Niagara* and soon made a positive identification. Almost at once the *Claymore*'s bow mooring parted, pulling the observation turret with Johnno inside down the slanting slope of the *Niagara*'s side-plating.

Approaching the ragged hole made by the mine, the diving bell jumped across the opening by luck, and saved Johnstone's life, for if the observation turret or bell had been caught in the hole, the wire connecting the turret to the *Claymore* would have snapped off, meaning suffocation for Johnstone.

On September 25 the strong room was exposed. Then further work severed the strong room door, but it fell in to the room rather than outside.

On October 13 a special grapple was sent down to move the strong room door out of the way. Soon the grapple sank its teeth into a wooden box inside the strong room. A short time later, the box fell on the deck of the recovery craft to reveal two massive gold ingots "each about a foot long, four inches wide, and an inch and a half thick, weighing thirty-four pounds."

By December 6 the operation was complete. Five hundred and fifty-five ingots out of 594, with a total value of ten million dollars, had been brought to the surface.

XXVII

Kidd Buried Treasure Here

Some years ago I took off from Norwood, Massachusetts, for a flight across Long Island Sound to Gardiner's Island in New York State. My companion, Bill Ashton, proved to be as interested in visiting the island as I obviously was. When he realized that we were heading for the spot where Captain William Kidd, the privateer, had actually buried treasure, he told me that one of his ancestors, Philip Ashton, had been captured by pirates back in 1722.

Soon after we had landed at the island airport, a landing field that consists more or less of rolling meadows, we were met by the island keeper who introduced himself as Charles A. Raynor. After securing the plane, we jumped aboard his truck and started for his house. As we drove along, we passed hundreds of osprey nests. Mr. Raynor told us about these interesting birds. There are about two thousand of them every spring, he said, and, though they are "monogamous," keeping the same mate year after year, they always return to the island singly.

The early history of Gardiner's Island is full of blood

and sacrifice. In fact, the Indian name of the island, Man-chonet, stands for "the place where many have died." There is a tradition that the island was sold to Lion Gardiner by Sachem Wyandanch in gratitude for his attempt to rescue Wyandanch's daughter from Ninigret, the Indian outlaw, during the Indian warfare on Long Island. During the Pequot Wars, Gardiner had been the one person who had kept the Connecticut and Massachusetts colonies from total destruction, and he felt perfectly equal to living on an island called "the place where many have died." He was fed up with the gross mismanagement of government on both sides of the ocean.

Gardiner's Island and the eastern end of Long Island at Montauk Point, where Sachem Wyandanch ruled, were never really affected by Indian warfare after Lion Gardiner came to the island. He seems to have had the personality and diplomacy which other English leaders lacked in dealing with the red man, and the Long Island Indians were free to come and go as they wished on his island.

In 1649 the settlement at Southampton was infuriated when an English woman was murdered and the Indians feared there would be a general reprisal against them. The settlers sent for Wyandanch. At the time Gardiner was visiting Sachem Wyandanch at his Montauk castle, and he offered to stay at Montauk as a hostage against Wyandanch's safe return. Fortunately, Wyandanch caught the murderers on his way to Southampton. They were Pequots from the mainland who were subsequently sent to Hartford to be tried and executed by the authorities there.

Charles Raynor, Bill Ashton, and I started out in a jeep to explore the island. Deer flashed by us unperturbed. Finally, we reached Kidd's Hollow, where a small granite marker tells us that Captain Kidd's treasure was "buried and recovered" in that hollow. Raynor and Ashton drove on ahead and I got out and walked around with the double intention of photographing ospreys close at hand and studying the famous hollow where Captain William Kidd himself had buried golden doubloons and pieces of eight.

Kidd's was quite a story, and after taking a few pictures of the ospreys in various attitudes of flight and nest-watching, I sat down in the hollow and leaned against a tree trunk to think it over.

When William Kidd anchored off Gardiner's Island in June 1699, John Gardiner, whose proprietorship extended from 1689 to 1738, was lord and master of the island. He was the eldest of the four children of David Gardiner, the second proprietor, and was known as a "hardy, active, robust man, generous and upright, rough in his manner, plain, agreeable to the manner of his time." Captain Kidd called on John Gardiner with an unusual request. In order to explain the reasons for this peculiar call it is necessary to give William Kidd's background and explain how he became one of the most wronged men in maritime history.

At the back of every great misunderstanding or legend there is always an event which has been warped by incorrect retelling until it no longer resembles the truth. One such misunderstanding is the current and common belief that Captain Kidd was a bloodthirsty buccaneer, killing men, women, and children, and scuttling ships wherever he went. He is known as the very symbol of piracy, and there is scarcely a cove or an island along the Atlantic Coast which is not said to contain a part of his "fabulous treasure." Falsehoods seem to prosper far more often than the truth, and I hope that by telling the real story of Captain Kidd I will help to balance the scales on the side of truth.

William Kidd was born in Scotland around 1654. Following the sea until 1691, he amassed a respectable fortune which allowed him to retire that same year. He was then known as William Kidd, gentleman. In May 1691, Kidd married a New York widow, Sarah Bradley Cort, and in 1695 traveled to London.

At that time Richard Coote, the Earl of Bellomont, was preparing to leave England as governor of both New England and New York. King William III was short of money, and Lord Bellomont suggested that a privateering expedition with broad powers granted and sponsored in part by the king himself would be a very lucrative venture.

Lord Bellomont suggested that a privateering expedition to the Red Sea would be especially profitable. There ships of the Great Mogul were sailing under passes given them by France, and they were easy prey. Captain William Kidd was suggested as the suitable leader of the expedition. When summoned before the king, Kidd showed little interest in the plan at first, but finally, because of Bellomont's persuasive manner, Kidd gave in and accepted the commission as the king's privateer against England's enemy, France. Eventually, the king, Bellomont, Kidd, and six other high government officials were included in the plan. Kidd sent forth under the Great Seal of England, on a partnership basis with the king himself!

The *Adventure Galley* was selected to serve as the ship for Kidd's adventure. Kidd sailed her to New York to augment his English crew and then headed for the Red Sea.

During the summer of 1697 a third of Kidd's crew of 155 died of cholera. The remainder were anxious to turn pirate but Kidd held them off and refused to board a friendly vessel which carried rich spoils. The crew was disgusted and would have mutinied if Kidd had not attacked their ringleader, Moore, the ship's gunner. The gunner later died of his injuries.

Soon after this misadventure, Kidd captured the *No-*

vembre, a Moorish vessel sailing under letters of marque from France. Kidd as a privateer demanded and received the French pass, resembling a letter of marque, thus exonerating himself from any charge of piracy.

In the winter of 1698, privateering Captain Kidd captured a rich prize, the *Quedah Merchant.* It proved to carry about $500,000 worth of rare silks, silver plate, jewels, pieces of eight and gold. After obtaining the captain's French pass, Kidd transferred his crew and goods to the *Quedah Merchant* and scuttled the *Adventure Galley.*

Meanwhile, in England, King William and the Whigs were forced to declare Kidd a pirate when the Tories exposed the secret partition treaty of 1698 which Kidd's partner, Lord Somers, had negotiated. This exposure revealed the use of the Great Seal of England on a personal privateering enterprise sponsored by the king. The Tories implicated Kidd and the king and others in the affair, until finally the king and his Whig adherents, to save themselves politically, sacrificed for all time Kidd's good name by declaring him a pirate.

As Captain Kidd made his triumphant trip to Boston, he stopped at several West Indian islands, including Nevis, Saint Thomas, and Antigua. At each port he learned that he had been declared a pirate. He sailed desperately from port to port like a hunted animal before he finally found a friend in Henry Bolton, an English trader who agreed to help him. Kidd's ship had begun to leak, and so for this and other reasons he decided to sail to Boston in a smaller vessel. After an exchange of goods, Bolton allowed Kidd to sail with the spoils from the *Quedah Merchant* aboard Bolton's six-gun sloop *Saint Antonio.*

And thus it was that Lord John Gardiner had a visit from Captain William Kidd in June 1699. On or about the twenty-eighth of June, Gardiner noticed the *Saint An-*

tonio riding at anchor off the island, and when the sloop was still there two days later Gardiner rowed out to investigate.

When Gardiner came aboard, Kidd explained that he was on his way to meet Lord Bellomont in Boston, and asked Gardiner if he could put ashore two Negro boys and a girl. The proprietor agreed. He had had previous experience with privateers and knew that it was useless to object. Two hours later, after the blacks were on the island, Kidd sent two bales of goods and a fourth Negro ashore.

The next morning the privateer requested and received a barrel of cider and six sheep. In return, he presented Gardiner with some damaged muslin and Bengal silk as a present for his wife. Soon afterward the sloop sailed away, firing four guns in salute.

Three days later Kidd returned and sent in to shore "a Chest and a box of Gold and a bundle of Quilts and four bales of Goods, which box of Gold the said Kidd told the Narrator was intended for Lord Bellomont." Two thirty-pound bags of silver and a small bundle of gold and gold dust were also put into Gardiner's keeping. The treasure was buried in Kidd's Hollow, and the *Saint Antonio* sailed away again. Later Kidd transferred two more treasure chests to his friend "Whisking" Clarke, leaving himself only enough gold and gold dust for expenses in Boston.

Meanwhile, a Mr. Emmott of New York was dispatched to Boston to discover what reception Kidd was likely to receive there. Bellomont, the man who had urged Kidd to undertake the expedition, was now to turn Judas and trick Kidd into going to Boston. He wrote a fine letter, assuring Kidd, among other things, that he would get him the King's pardon and pledging that "on my word and on my honor I will performe nicely what I have now promised."

Kidd, greatly relieved, went to Boston and roamed the streets freely for a week. At the end of the week, Governor Bellomont ordered him thrust into jail and later sent back to England. Bellomont kept Kidd's French passes from the Moorish vessels—Kidd's only proof that he was a privateer and not a pirate.

In England, Captain William Kidd was convicted of murder and sentenced to be hanged.

Until the very end, Kidd expected a reprieve. But on Friday, May 23, 1701, he was taken to Wapping-on-Thames and hanged from the scaffolding. The scaffolding broke as well as the rope and half an hour later his executioners used a nearby tree for their grim purpose. Kidd's body was later cut down and preserved with tar so that the mortal remains of the "wicked pirate" could be taken to a point near Tilbury Fort and suspended in public view.

In America, authorities soon confiscated all of the hoard Kidd had left on Gardiner's Island, as well as the chests in Whisking Clarke's custody and what few valuables had been found in Kidd's bedroom after his arrest. They even took Sarah Kidd's silver spoons, though she later recovered them. So the fabulous treasure which Kidd is alleged to have buried was reclaimed a few weeks after it was brought to Gardiner's Island, New York. The official list is carefully preserved in the British Archives. Every bit of treasure of every sort was carefully itemized and listed by a committee of six leading citizens. The spoils include the Gardiner's Island booty, what was found in Kidd's lodgings at Boston, and what was still aboard the sloop *Saint Antonio*. This most interesting document completely destroys the century-old myth concerning Captain Kidd—that his treasure is still to be found somewhere along the Atlantic Coast.

One reason why many people are confused as to the character of William Kidd and the nature of his visit to

Gardiner's Island is that eighty genuine pirates visited the island on September 2, 1728, causing great damage and much sorrow. The Boston *News-Letter* of September 19, 1728, tells us that owner John Gardiner was tied to a mulberry tree and severely cut; the family's beds were ripped open and the house was rifled of all silver except the famous Kidd tankard which Mrs. Gardiner carried as she fled. She and several other women were able to escape the island with the help of a faithful Indian who took them to Accabonack by canoe. An armed expedition was sent to Gardiner's Island at once, and the pirates fled the scene when their lookout sounded the alarm. They were Spanish and French pirates, high-seas desperadoes who roamed from Cuba to Maine, attacking both houses ashore and ships at sea.

XXVIII

Cocos Island

How many of the countless legends of Cocos Island are true? I am sure that by this late date it is difficult to separate accurate accounts from fictitious legends because for centuries Cocos has been visited by pirates, buccaneers, and sea rovers. In my opinion, the question of who buried treasure there and who did not will never be settled.

Many of the facts about Cocos Island have been misrepresented from earliest times. When we realize that there is another Cocos Island, sometimes called Cocos-Keeling, situated several hundred miles south of Java and often confused with the Cocos near Panama, it is easy to understand how some of the confusion has developed.

The Panama Cocos is about five miles long and six miles wide. Whatever your inclination may be after reading this chapter, think carefully before chartering plane or ship to get there, for it has been estimated that no less than four hundred expeditions have visited the island. All have failed to find treasure. A conservative estimate of the total expenses of the various expeditions made to Cocos through the years is over three million dollars, and so far less than a hundred dollars in coins have been taken from the island.

There are many tales connected with this isle. The first story concerns Captain William Kidd. The noted privateer is said to have visited the island and buried treasure there. By a strange coincidence, pirate Edward Davis also is rumored to have hidden several thousand pieces of eight and golden doubloons on Cocos. Later both men were lodged in the same jail at Boston, Massachusetts.

Benito Bonito, a notorious highwayman reported to have taken millions of dollars in gold and silver from the great treasure trains traveling from Mexico City toward the coast in the years 1819 and 1820, is supposed to have cached his great loot on Cocos Island in scores of kettles and trunks in the cliffs of Wafer Bay. In 1821 Bonito was said to have been captured by the British warship *Espiegle* and hanged.

The H.M.S. *Devonshire,* operating in these waters, was said to have captured many ships carrying treasure in 1821. Finally, according to the story, the British crew mutinied in the same year as Bonito's reputed death, took over the *Devonshire,* and sailed her to Cocos, where they are said to have buried the treasure.

The famed Loot of Lima is reported to be the largest of all the treasures hidden on Cocos. Over thirty-six million dollars in gold and silver were estimated to have been stored in a Lima church. At the time, Captain Marion Thompson was master of the schooner *Mary Dear,* then anchored in the Peruvian harbor. The residents of Lima awoke one morning to find that their gold and silver had vanished from the church, while the trim little schooner was also missing from the bay.

The story is that Captain Thompson sailed to Cocos Island, buried the treasure there, and sailed back to his

Newfoundland home. In the year 1844 he decided that enough time had elapsed since his theft to avoid being suspected of the crime, and he went to visit a Newfoundland sea captain named John Keating. Eventually, Thompson told Keating the entire story.

In turn, Keating interested a shipowner named Bogue, who promised to supply a vessel for a voyage to Cocos if he could share in the treasure.

One night, a month later, the three men were together in the home of Captain Keating. Thompson unrolled a chart of Cocos Island and pointed out to his fascinated friends the location of Chatham Bay there, explaining that they could steer the ship in between Nuez and Conic Islands to a safe anchorage. After they had finished their discussion, they took a drink of whiskey to seal their bond of friendship, and a moment later Thompson stood up suddenly.

"I'm done for," he gasped. "The curse of Cocos Island has got me!"

Ten minutes afterward, Thompson was dead. The two others stared at their late partner in horror, and then Keating ran to the village for the doctor, who returned with him.

"It was heart failure," the doctor explained. "He probably became too excited about something."

Some weeks after the funeral and the burial, the two survivors met again.

"Are you still willing to go ahead?" Keating asked Captain Bogue. The latter nodded in agreement.

Five months later their ship sighted Cocos Island, and the anchor rattled down in Chatham Bay. That week, according to their report, they actually located one of the four stores of wealth, but the excitement connected with the discovery was so great that it spread to the crew, who became unruly and demanded a proportional amount of the booty.

"We want our share now!" cried one particularly ugly sailor.

When Keating tried to quell the disturbance, the crew openly mutinied and went ashore in the yawl, refusing to return to the ship. But Keating and Bogue had been clever enough to cover over the treasure after finding it, and the men searched for a week, but in vain. Then, tired, hungry, and discouraged, the sailors rowed out to the ship one night and threatened Keating with death unless he revealed the location of the hoard.

Helpless to do otherwise, Captain Keating agreed to the demands of the mutineers and promised to go ashore with them at dawn. But that very night he and Bogue fled in the whaleboat and reached the island, determined to take the gold and hide it aboard ship, leaving the silver for the crew.

Luck was not with them. The two men reached shore without incident and loaded their money belts and treasure bags with doubloons, but when they arrived back at the beach a wind had come up. Although they launched their whaleboat successfully, the pair were unable to keep it into the wind and they capsized. Bogue, heavily loaded down with eighty-four pounds of gold, never came to the surface, but Keating, who carried his gold in a sack, released his treasure and clung to the gunnel of the boat. The whaleboat drifted by the end of the island, and two days later Keating was picked up at sea.

Back at Cocos, the mutineers searched unsuccessfully for several more weeks and then sailed back to their home port where they fled the craft at once.

It was twenty years before Keating decided to try again. This time he interested a man named Nicholas Fitzgerald in the new project. Keating had married a very young girl, and she was fascinated by the charts, maps, and directions which her husband had saved. As in the case of Captain Thompson years before, however, Keating died suddenly in the midst of preparations to leave on this next venture.

In the year 1893 a Mrs. Richard Young of Boston announced that she was the daughter of Keating and was planning an expedition to Cocos Island, as she had all of the precious treasure maps of the Newfoundland treasure seeker. A group was organized under the leadership of Captain William Hackett, and they sailed away from Boston on the brig *Aurora.* Trouble began almost at once, and because of it the expedition turned around for home while still hundreds of miles away from the island.

About 1893 the island was visited by a German explorer named Von Bremer. He spent a small fortune tunneling through cliffs and mountains, but found nothing. Also on the island around this period was an unusual gentleman named Gissler, who assumed the title of governor of Cocos, getting his authority from Costa Rica. Governor Gissler remained at Cocos for twenty years, and as far as is known never unearthed anything except a Spanish doubloon dated 1788, which is said to have been acquired by the late treasure-minded author Charles B. Driscoll of New York.

Incidentally William Kidd never came within one thousand miles of Cocos Island, and so naturally he could not have buried treasure there. Nor is it on record anywhere that his cellmate, Edward Davis, buried either gold or silver at Cocos.

Also, there is no proof that Bonito buried treasure at Cocos. Neither is there evidence that he was captured or hanged by the crew aboard the British warship *Espiegle* in 1821 or any other year.

In the case of the *Devonshire,* this craft was not even in

250 Ghosts, Gales and Gold

commission in the year 1821 when her sailors were said to
have mutinied and buried treasure at Cocos.

Finally, not one of the many writers who mention the
incident of Captain Thompson and the *Mary Dear* admits
having done research work to see if the man or the ship
ever existed. Actually, there never was a Captain Thompson of that period who visited Cocos Island, no one by that
name ever had a vessel called the *Mary Dear*, and neither
he nor anyone else ever took the so-called Loot of Lima.
The records at Lima reveal no robbery of that sort at the
time.

Of course, if you still feel that there is treasure at Cocos
Island, by all means visit there and dig to your heart's content. And, should you discover a fabulous amount of gold
or silver, rest assured it is not the treasure for which so
many have searched. No, you will have unearthed an entirely new, unknown cache, and I'll be the first to con-
gratulate you—when you find it.

Index